TIM HEALD

Business Unusual

PAN BOOKS
in association with
Macmillan London

First published 1989 by Macmillan London Limited
This edition published 1991 by Pan Books Ltd,
Cavaye Place, London SW10 9PG
in association with Macmillan London
1 3 5 7 9 8 6 4 2
© Tim Heald 1989
ISBN 0 330 31588 9

Printed in England by Clays Ltd, St Ives plc

Business Unusual

Tim Heald, heterosexual suburban male with original wife, is a journalist, past chairman of the Crime Writers' Association, secretary of International PEN, novelist and biographer.

He is a fanatical real tennis player, enjoys all spectator sports, food, talk, drink and travel.

PROLOGUE

'Fellow members of the Scarpington Artisans' Lodge, Your Graces, My Lord, ladies and gentlemen . . .' Reg Brackett, MBE (for community services), picked nervously at his chain of office and flashed his dentures at the assembled company. One hundred and seventy-three souls were crammed into the King Alfred the Great Banqueting Room at the three-star Talbot Hotel, flagship of the Jolly Trencherman chain, owned by Scarpington's most successful son, Sir Seymour Puce, MP for the city, who was seated on the left of the Countess of Scarpington herself. Black-tied Artisans and their wives were augmented by the great and good of Scarpington and District. The Earl of Scarpington, Grand Patron of the Lodge, was guest of honour and would speak next. The Bishop of Scarpington had said the traditional Artisans' Grace ('For these thy gifts, the fruits of thy mercy and of our dutiful toil and labour, we thank thee, Lord') and they had all scoffed their way through the Fruit Cocktail Artisan, the Baron of Beef Scarpington and the Coupe Talbot.

Now the nose-powdering break was over, the port was on the table and this year's President of the Artisans was on his feet. It was not so much that Reg was unaccustomed to public speaking, more that he didn't seem to be able to get the hang of it. He had raided hundreds of Gyles Brandreth joke books, knew every Englishman, Scotsman, Irishman and Welshman story in the world and could even manage sexy racism – though he tended to keep that for stag nights. Despite this, or perhaps because of it, his after-dinner speeches were literally stunning.

All round the King Alfred Room men and women looked

duly stunned. The strong drinks before dinner coupled with the Blue Nun and the Nuits-St-Georges had a lot to do with this, but so did Reg. As Chairman and Chief Executive of Bracketts Laundry and Dry Cleaning Services (Est. 1936) Reg was a force in the land. Had he not been a force in the land he would not, naturally, have been President of the Artisans. The Artisans of Scarpington were to the Masons or the Rotary as the Brigade of Guards to the Pioneer Corps. They were an élite. Of course Scarpington had its Round Table and its Guild of Scarpington Men, but they were as New Zealand Cheddar to Stilton. Membership of the Scarpington Artisans' Lodge was what all good burghers of Scarpington wished for themselves. To be an Artisan was to have arrived. They were, paradoxically, the salt of Scarpington and its cream as well.

All along the top table sat the predecessors of President Brackett. Brown of Brown's Dairy; Green of Green and Green, Builders Merchants; Sinclair of Sinclair's who made custom-built invalid carriages and had once held the warrant for the Royal House of Iraq; Festing of Festing, Festing, Hackett, Festing and Festing, the top solicitors in town; Moulton of Moulton and Bragg, the brewers of Scarpington Special; Fothergill, owner and proprietor of the *Scarpington Times* (incorporating the *Scarpington Clarion and Faringay Echo*).

They were all there with their wives; all plump with dinner and self-importance; all nodding off quietly almost in time to Brackett's post-prandial drone.

As the speech wore on, it seemed to those very few who were paying close attention that Reg's speech was becoming more than usually slurred and his delivery more than usually faltering. He told the story about the Englishman, the Scotsman and the Irishman on the desert island with even less than his customary panache.

'So the Englishman says to the genie, "Take me back to Blighty"; and the genie claps his hands and the Englishman vanishes.' The Earl of Scarpington's head fell on to his chest and he breathed very heavily for a moment before shaking himself awake like an ancient Sealyham coming in from the rain. 'And the Scotsman says to the genie, "Take me back to Glasgie"; and the genie claps his hands and the Scotsman vanishes.'

Brown glanced at Green and winked; Fothergill looked at Festing and raised an eyebrow; Sinclair stifled a yawn.

Reg Brackett's voice was beginning to sound like an old gramophone record fast running down.

'And finally,' he said, 'the genie asks the Irishman for his wish and the Irishman says . . .'

Almost everyone present had heard Reg tell the story at the Scarpington Scarecrows Cricket Club Annual Dinner and Dance in this very room less than a month earlier, so they all knew what the Irishman's wish was. But this time the wish was never articulated for just as Reg was about to tell everyone what it was his eyes, which had almost shut, suddenly opened very wide and revolved briefly. There was a momentary gargling sound and he fell forward with startling rapidity, smashing a port glass with his forehead and ending face down on the table where he lay quite still.

He was, of course, extremely dead.

CHAPTER ONE

The Bognors and Business

It did not seem a good idea, even at the time.

'The business of the Board of Trade, Bognor, is "trade",' said Parkinson at their weekly meeting. His boss glowered out from beneath the reproduction of Annigoni's portrait of the Queen, looking, thought Bognor, sadly frayed at the edges. A lifetime of civil service was poor preparation for a fulfilling retirement, and Parkinson, now in his early sixties, was beginning to look as if he might not even make it. Bognor guessed that it was only the prospect of some sort of valedictory gong that was keeping him in harness. Parkinson OBE. The Officers of the Order of the British Empire ranked immediately below Members of the Fourth Class of the Royal Victorian Order and two above the eldest sons of the younger sons of peers. Bognor knew this because he had been told by his wife's great-aunt Celia many years before. The information had stuck in the irritating way that worthless information so often did. Bognor smiled at the idea of old Parky ranking above the eldest sons of the younger sons of peers. The thought that OBE was traditionally supposed to stand for 'Other Buggers' Efforts' and that in this instance he was the principal 'other bugger' widened the smile. Parkinson, not pleased, tried to wipe it smartly from Bognor's face.

'It may seem funny to you, sunshine,' he said, 'but it's life and death to most of us. Britain is a nation of grocers, and don't you forget it.'

'Shopkeepers, actually,' said Bognor mildly, 'or, to quote

with precision, "boutiquiers". Only I don't think Napoleon meant "boutique" in the modern sense, there being no Carnaby Street in his day. Or not in the sense that we understand it.'

Parkinson's pencil, with which he had been jabbing his blotter, snapped, and he swore.

'Don't try on that sort of smart-alec pseudo-intellectualism with me, Bognor,' he said. 'You may not have noticed, but this country has returned to good old-fashioned Victorian values. That's what Thatcher's about.'

'Grocering,' said Bognor. 'God made the wicked grocer . . . that's what Thatcher's about. Poisoning us all with cut-price corned beef.'

Parkinson thrust his ruined pencil into the blotter, rose to his feet and told Bognor not to be silly. Then, making a severe effort to appear reasonable and efficient in the manner expected of a senior Board of Trade person hanging on for a middle-range medal on retirement, he said, 'The fact of the matter is, Bognor, that we don't know enough about . . . well, about a place like, well . . .' he stabbed at the map of England alongside the Annigoni print, 'places like . . . Scarpington.'

Long pause. Very long pause, deepening into very long pause indeed, and fast shading into a silence of genuine incomprehension.

Finally Bognor broke it in the only way he could think of – a trick he had heard was often employed by royalty when flummoxed. Prince Philip, he understood, on being introduced to, let us say, an orthodontist, will ask 'What do you do?' The orthodontist will reply, 'I am an orthodontist' to which Prince Philip will say, 'Ah, an orthodontist', thus delivering what rugby players call a 'hospital pass' straight back to the orthodontist.

'Scarpington,' said Bognor.

'Scarpington,' said Parkinson and they glared at each other.

It was Parkinson who capitulated. His fuse was shortening in old age.

9

'Scarpington', he said, 'is middle England. It's what politicians talk about and newspapers write about, but no MP ever goes there and nor does any journalist unless there's a particularly juicy murder. It's unfashionable but it's vital. It's as unknown to your average Whitehall mandarin as the rain forest of Cameroon or the Kalahari Desert. It's a vote-winner; it's a bread-winner; it's what this country is all about. But no one down here in the corridors of power even begins to understand it. It's deeply unfashionable and hideously boring and they've not heard of Australian Chardonnay or late Picasso. It's a dump, Bognor. Not your sort of place at all. But it's where most of the God-forsaken people in this God-forsaken country live and breathe and sweat and toil and provide the prosperity that allows the privileged few to take three-hour lunches and a long weekend. Our masters, Bognor, need to know more about this place and, as a first step, they have decided, in their infinite wisdom, to send you there. To Scarpington, which is the most middling place in the whole of middle England. You are going to Scarpington and you are not coming back until you can tell us what makes it tick. You may take your wife.'

There was no arguing with this and Bognor knew it. Such lyricism only took Parkinson once every year, usually, he had observed, at about the time of the summer solstice. When it descended upon him like the gift of tongues it was best not to argue.

Bognor, of course, had no experience of Scarpington nor of those myriad places like it. As far as he was concerned, no one went there and no one came from there. It was a blank on the map, a no-man's-land in every sense of the word. A thought suddenly struck him. There had been a man at Oxford, Teddy Hall, he rather thought, a secretary or treasurer of the University Gastronomes, who, on being asked, as one always was, where one had been at school, replied, 'Er . . . Scarpington, actually.' He had been very dim.

'Pack your bags, my sweet,' he said that evening to his long-suffering spouse. 'We're off to Scarpington. For a stay of indefinite duration.'

'You what?' Monica's mouth puckered.

'Scarpington.'

'I heard you. Mediaeval minster; minor public school; undistinguished stately home; light industry, some antiquated, some state of the art; perfect example of the England nobody knows about but everybody cites as a vital reference; there's a particularly good Saxon archway at a church called, I think, St Botolph-without-the-wall; and Pevsner was moderately keen on the town hall; conservative with big and small "c".'

Bognor's eyes widened. He poured himself a more than usually stiff Scotch.

'Have you been talking to Parkinson?'

'Of course not.' Monica had a good line in scorn even when she was only demonstrating an above-average expertise in a peculiarly English variant of Trivial Pursuit.

'But how do you know so much about it?'

'It's the sort of thing one knows. And yes, please, I'd like a drink too.'

He poured her one. Not quite as stiff as his.

'To be fair,' she said, 'some cousins of my mother came from somewhere near there. He was a country vicar in some benighted coal-mining community not far away. They talked about Scarpington as if it was the Great Wen.'

'Ah.' Bognor was relieved. His wife's ability to know more than he did about so many things was a source of perpetual irritation, and it was some solace to find that in this particular instance she had, in effect, been cheating.

'There seems,' he said, 'to be a widely held view that Scarpington is one of those places where "real" people come from.'

'That sounds like politician's-speak.' Monica grinned. 'We're talking about the "silent majority", are we not? People who vote in elections and are canvassed in opinion polls.'

'Probably. Only this time it's being tarted up as the economic heart of the nation. The theory is that the country's wealth does not derive from North Sea Oil or boardroom intrigue or even new City spivvery but from thrift and graft in places like Scarpington.'

Monica smiled more widely, showing strong, irregular, equine teeth. 'The Grantham Grocer theory of economics.'

'Precisely.'

'And you are to produce a Board of Trade memorandum demonstrating how it works in practice.'

'In a nutshell.'

'In that case,' said Monica, 'I think you'd better take me out for a decent meal. As Edwina Currie keeps telling us, there's nothing to eat north of the Trent except for chip butties.'

Thus it was that the Bognors came to Scarpington. For Bognor it was just part of life's poor hearthrug. Since he had first inadvertently wandered into the Special Investigations Department of the Board of Trade all those long long years ago after the ridiculous muddle at the University Appointments Board, he had often thought of escaping. But he had been too lazy. Of course he was stuck in a rut, as Monica and his cousins and aunts and friends and contemporaries all told him. And what, pray, was so wrong in that? Looking round at the world of the middle-aged, which was where he now found himself, he reckoned he was very privileged to have a rut in which to be stuck. There were worse places to be. He had a roof over his head; a modest expense account; a pension scheme, index linked. There was even the possibility of early retirement before too terribly long.

Looking back on the water that had flowed under his particular bridge he had to admit that it had been a bit of a trickle, that the early promise had not really been fulfilled. But *what* promise, one had to ask oneself? Had there been any genuine promise? A poem in the college magazine. A place at Oxford. A less than dazzling performance as Cornwall in *Lear* ('Out, vile jelly! Where is thy lustre now?'). One or two moderate school reports. It did not add up to a tremendously exciting promise, and if one were absolutely honest one had to admit that the only person who had even momentarily thought that he was going to become rich and famous was his dear mother, and even she was never truly convinced.

Bognor sighed. He really shouldn't have let himself go quite so badly to seed. He should never have given up exercise, though if he was honest with himself he had to admit that there had never really been any exercise to give up. And in his mid-forties, carrying at least two stone too much weight and smoking cheroots and drinking alcohol the way he did it would be folly to turn to exercise now. Certain disaster. Jogging kills. He knew it. And really it was too late to give up smoking and drinking. The withdrawal would undoubtedly lead to stress which would damage the heart. Much better carry on as he was, even though it would be nice not to . . . well, Monica was right. He did 'wobble' rather these days and if he wore trousers and a belt the effect was 'unedifying' though it was not kind of Monica to put it quite like that. There was no point in trying to look younger than one's age and if a chap was middle-aged a chap should accept it and grow middle-aged gracefully. Gracefully was the wrong adverb. Redundant, though, like most adverbs. It was Graham Greene who made such a fetish of adverbs. He had read that in an interview recently. At least he still read quite a bit. He might be a bit sluggish physically but his mind was still rippling with muscle. It made one surprisingly attractive to women still. It was interesting to find how intelligent, mature women were attracted by a good mind.

Like Monica. Monica was middle-aged too, but it suited her. Those horsy looks which had made her seem gangling and clumsy as a young woman, all knees and elbows, were positively elegant now that she had just turned forty. There was a little grey at the temples which she refused to tamper with and she had interesting lines at the mouth and the corners of her eyes. They imparted character and it was character that had always been her strong point. He was very lucky to have Monica. She was a chum.

He was reflecting thus, in an uncharacteristic way, self-analysis and introspection not being particular foibles of his, when Reg Brackett keeled over into his port.

For a moment there was a silence, a lack of noise as 173 people seemed to hold their breath, which was positively eerie. Then the moment was past, there was a general exhalation and a rhubarbing hubbub of chatter, through which the voice of Sir Seymour Puce cut like a spoon through the Coupe Talbot.

'A doctor,' he shouted, with the authority of a man born to rule. 'A doctor. Doctor Dick, Doctor Dick, come to the top table at once.'

From somewhere well below the salt a small, bald, freckle-faced person started to push his way through the assembled diners.

Bognor glanced across at his wife who was sitting on the other side of his table two places down. They exchanged looks which could not have been interpreted by an outsider but which said, in unison, 'Oh God, here we go again.'

They had only been in Scarpington for three days, yet here already was the first corpse. Both knew, intuitively, that Reg Brackett was already a stiff. It happened too too terribly often. An ordinary routine enquiry in an ordinary routine sort of place and then quite without warning and totally against the run of play someone died. In this particular instance it looked like a common or garden thrombosis brought on by an excess of food, drink and after-dinner speechifying. Oddly enough, Bognor had made a tour of Bracketts Laundry and Dry Cleaning Services that very afternoon, personally conducted by the President of Artisans himself. Bognor had thought then that Reg had seemed oddly jumpy, but he had put it down to pre-dinner nerves. The Artisans' dinner was a grand affair and daunting for a laundryman and dry cleaner no matter how eminent.

The doctor reached the slumped Reg, loosened collar and cuffs, then felt for a pulse. Bognor and Monica, like everyone else in the room, tried to see what was happening without, somehow, being seen to look. A typical British predicament. Bognor felt like telling the quack not to waste his time. A woman, presumably Mrs Brackett, was sobbing noisily and was led away by two others. A small crowd of top-table dignitaries gathered round the corpse.

Now the toastmaster took a hand, banging his gavel with three mighty whacks.

'Your Grace, My Lord, ladies and gentlemen,' he bawled, half-way between Pavarotti and a Guards drill sergeant. 'Pray silence for the Rt Honourable Sir Seymour Puce, Member of Parliament for Scarpington.'

Sir Seymour was – very unusually for him – brief and to the point.

'Dinner's over,' he said. 'No more speeches, but the bars stay open till half eleven. I know Reg wouldn't want to interfere with anyone's fun but we'd like the room cleared as quick as possible. Sorry about the curtailment. Good night and God bless!'

A general scuffing back of chairs greeted this announcement. Bognor walked round to his wife.

'Drink?' he said.

'I don't see why not. We don't have to drive anywhere.'

This was true. The Bognors were putting up at the Talbot. Their room was not exactly splendiferous but it was the best hotel in town. Staying there gave Bognor a status he would have been pushed to pretend to if he had gone to the bed-and-breakfast suggested by Parkinson. Parkinson was motivated by penny-pinching, pardonable in view of pressure from above, and a desire to humiliate his subordinate, which was unpardonable from any perspective whatever.

The main bar of the Talbot was labelled the St Moritz, partly because St Moritz carried connotations of class which a three-star hotel in a little-known middling English city badly needed and partly because Sir Seymour had, in early middle age, taken to holidaying in the Alps and going down the Cresta Run. His *Who's Who* entry included 'Cresta Run' under Recreations and 'St Moritz Tobogganing' under Clubs. He thought this smart. So did many of his self-made colleagues on the Tory back benches. He was not aware that those whose smartness he really envied were inclined to snigger.

Naming the bar after that prestigious – in every sense – Alpine watering hole had no effect whatever. The bar was still known throughout Scarpington and the surrounding district as Freddie's, after the head barman, who had been an institution for more than thirty years and appeared, to Sir Seymour's irritation, to be unsackable. Freddie was never entirely sober and yet had never been seen to be quite drunk. Like many barmen he was a sympathetic and discreet receiver of confidences and an occasional dispenser, if not of wisdom, of tips and inside information relating to the 2.30 at Haydock and the immediate prospects of South American tin on the market. He was probably Scarpington's leading Mr Fixit and he knew more of the city's private life than any Scarpingtonian alive. He could have made a comfortable living from blackmail, but chose not to.

Freddie's bar had undergone a modest tarting up when the Jolly Trencherman chain acquired the Talbot from the private company headed by the Earl of Scarpington. There had been a ferocious boardroom battle over that and the Earl and Sir Seymour had been the best of enemies ever since. The Earl had even resigned his presidency of the Conservative Association. The old flock wallpaper had been replaced with tasteful beige and cream stripes; the gilt bracket lamps had made way for concealed spots; and the hunting and sporting prints had been replaced by Alpine and tobogganing scenes. For a few weeks it had almost lived up to this new image, but Freddie, in his stained maroon jacket and ill-tied black bow, knew that part of the secret of his bar's success was its sleaze. Before long he had managed to make the St Moritz as louche and grubby as it had been in the old days when there had simply been Gothic print on the door saying 'Bar'.

Within moments of Sir Seymour's perfunctory closure of proceedings Freddie's bar was full to the gills with Artisans and their wives. The Artisans, for the most part, ordered beer or Scotch while their wives drank lager and lime or bitter lemon. Perrier had made a hesitant appearance in Scarpington at a young people's wine and pick-up bar called the Brasserie Donovan. Badoit was still unknown.

Bognor and Monica found themselves pressed hard against Harold Fothergill of the *Scarpington Times*. Mrs Fothergill was also part of the scrum. Fothergill was almost the first person on whom Bognor had called. He was a slight, ferrety figure who had inherited the paper from his father. Father was of an old school, given to green eye-shades, carpet slippers, braces and a dank, half-smoked cigar permanently anchored to the middle of his mouth. He could still be found lurking about the *Times* office, complaining about the new technology installed by his trendy son.

'Well, it's Mr Bognor,' he said, elbowing his way towards the bar. 'May I buy you a drink? This is my wife, Edna.'

Edna smiled, sourly. Her husband looked like a man with a roving eye. He gave Monica a smile which Bognor considered lecherous.

'Thanks,' said Bognor. 'I'll have a pint of Old Parsnip.' This was Moulton and Bragg's strongest, most expensive and most real. 'This is my wife, Monica.'

'Nice to meet you, Monica,' said Harold, somehow managing to grab a hand and kissing it. Monica seemed unimpressed and said she'd like a Hine cognac.

'Why don't you girls find a quiet space in a corner?' said Harold, 'and we'll get the drinks and join you.'

The girls did as they were told, though there seemed no reasonable prospect of finding such a thing as a quiet corner.

'Reg looked dead to me,' hissed Harold, when the wives were out of earshot.

'I wasn't close enough to see properly,' said Bognor, 'but there didn't seem much sign of movement.'

'He smoked too much and he lived on his nerves.' The man in front turned round with two fistfuls of drink and barged past. Harold dived into the gap and tugged Bognor in with him. 'Evening, Fred!' he said to the barman, who nodded in the lugubrious, timeworn manner he always

17

affected. 'Two Parsnips, a large Hine and a ginger wine, when you've got a moment.'

He turned back to Bognor.

'Entre-nous,' he hissed into Bognor's right ear, 'things hadn't been going too well at the laundry. There was talk.'

'Talk?'

'Customs and Excise were having a hard look at the books. Or so my spies tell me. And there were one or two of the big boys nosing around. Mr Clean and Bleach'n'Starch to name but two.'

Freddie came back with the drinks.

'Sorry to hear about Mr Brackett,' he said, accepting Fothergill's proffered tenner. 'Very sudden.'

'Very sudden,' said the Editor. 'Didn't even have time to deliver the punch-line.'

'You mean Mr Clean and Bleach'n'Starch were thinking of a takeover?' asked Bognor. 'He didn't say anything about it to me. Not even by implication.'

'Well, he wouldn't, would he? He probably thought you were doing a snoop on behalf of the VATmen.'

'I'm Board of Trade,' said Bognor with asperity. 'Nothing whatever to do with VAT. That's Customs and Excise. Quite a different matter.'

Mr Fothergill narrowed his eyes. 'It's all government,' he said. 'Those of us in the Fourth Estate tend to lump all you boys together. It may seem unreasonable to you, but for a committed, responsible journalist it has to be a question of Them and Us. I'm "us" and you're "them".'

'I see,' said Bognor, accepting a pint tankard and a brandy balloon.

'Don't get me wrong,' said Fothergill. 'Some of my best friends are in government, but it has to be an adversarial relationship. Doesn't mean to say you can't meet over a meal or a drink, but fundamentally we have different aims.'

'I'm not sure I entirely agree.' Bognor started to shove his way back through the throng of Artisans. 'But then I'm an essentially non-confrontational sort of person. I like compromise. A quiet life. I'm sure we all want the same thing in the end.'

'You people all say that,' said Fothergill, sipping the froth off his Parsnip to stop it spilling on their way to the quiet corner, 'but when the chips are down it just ain't true.'

They hit a patch of relatively open space.

'You were saying, though' – Bognor was aware that they had been diverted – 'that Brackett was in trouble. And a takeover target.'

'I have a well-placed friend at Bleach'n'Starch,' said Fothergill. 'Let's just say that when they had a run through the books they weren't happy with what they found.'

'Is that a fact?'

'No.' Fothergill smiled. 'If it was a fact the *Times* would have printed it. But my guess is that it's probably true. And if you really are interested in the truth about trade here in Scarpington I think you'd do well to have a word with your friends at Customs and Excise about the affairs of Bracketts Laundry.'

They rejoined the ladies who had found a relatively quiet haven under a portrait of the first Lord Brabazon of Tara.

Monica was, implausibly, giving Mrs Fothergill the gist of her way of dealing with squid – a light rolling sauté in chateau-bottled olive oil with chopped shallot, red chilli, and garlic, finished off with a splash of white Rioja. Mrs Fothergill did not give the impression of dealing much with squid herself and Bognor had a strong sense of a subject newly changed.

He wondered what.

'Well,' said Fothergill, raising his glass and getting Parsnip froth in his moustache, 'here's to poor old Reg.'

'I liked Reginald,' said Mrs Fothergill.

'Liked?' Her husband eyed her with what looked like disbelief.

'Yes, liked. I was fond of him. He was a nice man.'

'Why the past tense?'

Mrs Fothergill sighed. 'You saw him, Harold. He's in the past tense. Poor man was white and limp as a codfish. He's not alive any longer.'

This was, the Bognors knew, true. Reg had gone to God, to the Great Round Table in the Sky, to the Ultimate Laundry where everything and everybody were whiter than white. As Edna Fothergill suggested, there was no more life in him than in a fish finger. Bognor remembered the terrible old school pun which lumbered out every Friday lunch, the one about the piece of cod which passeth all understanding. It was bad that his mind turned to flippancies at moments like this, moments of death and drama where a gentleman was supposed, in a metaphorical manner of speaking, to remove his hat and place it over his heart while standing to attention.

'Edna, whatever else he is – or may have been – Reg Brackett is – or was - *not* a nice man. If he *has* survived, his prospects of becoming nice are non-existent!'

'Come along now, Fothergill, *De mortuis nil nisi bonum.* Brackett may be dead but he's not even cold yet, much less buried. Bit of respect, if you please.'

The speaker was Sir Seymour Puce who now stood four-square before them, a magnificently solid presence, all jowels and jangling watch chains.

'So he *is* dead?'

Monica fixed the Member for Scarpington with one of her beadiest.

Puce glared back. Hate at first sight.

'I don't believe I've had the pleasure,' he said.

Nor likely to, thought Bognor, admiring, not for the first time, his wife's forthright manner.

'Monica Bognor,' said Monica, 'and this is my husband Simon. Of the Board of Trade. Whitehall.'

'Special Investigations Department, actually,' said Simon, offering a hand which Sir Seymour did not take.

'I heard someone from Whitehall had been ferreting around,' he said. 'Yes, Madam, I'm afraid Mr Brackett has gone to join his maker. Fothergill, I'll be writing a tribute

20

myself. You shall have it by lunch tomorrow. Five hundred words. You'll carry a photograph, of course. Three columns at least, but an inside page. Brief news story on the front. "President of Artisans passes away after masterful oration". You know the sort of thing. Now I have business to attend to. Delighted to have met you, Mrs Bognor. You too, Mr Bognor.'

And he was gone as speedily and totally as he had come.

'I didn't realise Puce ran the *Times*,' said Bognor before his wife could stop him.

Harold Fothergill looked thunderous. 'He doesn't,' he said.

You could have fooled me, thought Bognor, but this time he kept the sentence to himself. Tact was not his strongest suit, but he could see that any intimation that Fothergill was not the Murdoch of his own newspaper would be ill received. Nevertheless it gave him pause for thought.

It was obvious that Puce was a bully, but it took two to be bullied. Interesting to find that Fothergill made a pair with Puce – particularly as Fothergill so obviously bullied poor Edna.

They drank up and left.

CHAPTER TWO

The Bognors at Breakfast

'You're being gratuitously melodramatic.' Monica eyed the runny yolk of her fried egg and debated the odds against salmonella. Dammit, she liked egg yolks and she was in the prime of life. It was only infants and the old who died of it, anyway.

A thought struck her.

'Maybe he'd eaten a bad egg.'

'There were no eggs on the menu.' Bognor was trying to dissect a kipper without much success. It was a dried-out bit of fish, overcooked and, even by the standards of kippers, excessively bony.

'A very slow acting egg,' said his wife. 'A time bomb of an egg. Perhaps he ate it for breakfast but it didn't go off till after dinner.'

'It would have to be off when he ate it,' said Bognor. 'It can't go off once you've eaten it.'

'Time bomb, stupid. "Off", as in bomb . . . explosion . . . bang. Not as in egg . . . rotten.'

Bognor shook his head and eyed *The Independent* which led with a story about opinion polls. He read the headline twice but couldn't understand it any more than his wife's wittering. Ambiguities confused him these days. The advancing years demanded black and white simplicity.

'I don't care what you think,' he said. 'My view is that Brackett was done in. And I think the post-mortem will prove it. But there's no point in arguing. It'll all come out when they analyse the contents of his stomach. Or whatever.'

'Simon, please. Not at breakfast.' The egg yolk had been runnier than she had realised. Swallowing it was not an altogether happy sensation. 'There's absolutely no reason to suppose Brackett was done in, as you so elegantly put it. It's perfectly straightforward. Happens all the time. He was obviously overweight. Drank too much. Quite possibly smoked. Worked himself up into a fearful paddy over that ridiculous speech and "pouf!" the old ticker simply couldn't take the strain.'

She allowed a gnarled waitress in a black outfit with a white pinny to remove her plate, then buttered and marmaladed some thin, charred toast.

'I didn't know you were an expert on cardiac arrest,' said Bognor, buttering his own toast.

'I only know what I read in the colour supplements,' said Monica. 'And common sense. I'd watch it yourself, if I were you. You're beginning to look gross.'

'I'm perfectly safe,' said Bognor. 'I haven't made an after-dinner speech in over twenty years.'

'Don't be ridiculous,' she said. 'I meant the butter. And not taking any exercise.'

'Now exercise *would* kill me,' said Bognor. 'And I am not being ridiculous. You were the one who said Brackett was killed by after-dinner speaking. I'm surprised more people didn't die, in that case. It was boring enough.'

'That's in extremely bad taste.'

'Yes,' said Bognor, abandoning the kipper. 'Extremely.'

Husband and wife glowered at each other in a silence interrupted a minute or so later by Henry, the head waiter, a functionary of the old, that is to say geriatric, school of head waitering. He was on the verge of retirement and replacement by his number two, Carlo, who was of a newer persuasion. Henry had taken a definite shine to Monica.

'Excuse me, sir, madam,' he said. 'There's a gentleman to see you.'

'A gentleman?' Bognor was momentarily nonplussed. 'To see me?'

'Oh, for God's sake!' Monica, unlike her husband, had all

her wits about her at breakfast. 'Don't be such a blancmange. Send him in, Henry.'

Henry beamed, departed and re-emerged into the simmering silence with a small, middle-aged man whose plain clothes were as much of a uniform as a uniform could be.

'Wartnaby,' he said, flashing a smile and laminated ID. 'CID. Mind if I join you?'

This was unexpected. Bognor usually had trouble with the police. His experience of them was that they were everything that was alleged – uncouth, plodding and boorish at best; corrupt, bigoted and racist at worst. As he was not good at concealing this prejudice, his relationship with the law invariably got off to a bad start. Policemen tended to regard him as supercilious and slothful. This man Wartnaby, however – Detective Chief Inspector Wartnaby – seemed, apart from his suit, to be of a different order altogether.

'Of course not,' said Bognor. 'I'm Bognor. This is Monica. Have a coffee.'

'Heard a lot about you from your chief, Parkinson.'

'Ah.' Bognor's hand, poised above the handle of the coffee pot, paused. Hearing things from the boss was not good. Wartnaby may have started by speaking with a silvery tongue, but if he had been listening to Parkinson it would almost certainly turn out to be forked.

'He was very nice about you, actually,' said Wartnaby, 'though most of the time we discussed his lecture.'

'Lecture?' Bognor poured.

'On Chelsea.'

'Chelsea.' Bognor repeated the word inanely. He was groping. The Board of Trade had no particular cases in Chelsea, not that he could remember. Oh, wait a minute, antiques. Bognor cudgelled the brain ferociously. Export licences, the ring, dodgy Hepplewhites, it was all coming back.

'Porcelain,' said Wartnaby. 'I collect miniature scent bottles and your man Parkinson came to lecture to the Scarpington Antiquarian Society on Nicholas Sprimont. He's supposed to be working on a biography, as you probably know.'

'I didn't,' said Bognor, shocked. This called for a major revision of his opinion of Parkinson. In all their chequered history together – the best part of twenty years now – he had never heard Parkinson express any sentiment in any way suggestive of what one might term cultural 'bottom'. Bognor had always thought of him, in aesthetic, cultural and intellectual terms, as little better than a policeman. And to make matters more difficult here was a detective chief inspector who collected scent bottles. What on earth was happening to the world of detection and forensics? There'd be policemen writing poetry and going to the opera before you knew where you were.

'Well, there you are,' said Wartnaby. 'One never really knows the people one thinks one knows best. In any case, we had a little talk after the lecture and he said you'd be coming up to have a look at "middle England".'

Monica favoured him with a smile stiff with the superiority of the suburban south-east.

Wartnaby smiled back with a relaxed flash of well-maintained, mildly irregular teeth which said in body language that he was going to have no problem remaining on at least equal terms with the Bognors or anybody else thrown up by Whitehall and all its works.

'Parkinson didn't say anything to me about a porcelain lecture. Or about you, come to that.' Bognor was not trying to seem disobliging. It just came out like that.

Wartnaby did not seem to think this required comment so he waited until Bognor, wishing to make up for having been abrupt said, 'But it's very nice to see you.'

'I gather you were at last night's dinner,' said Wartnaby. He was not drinking his coffee.

The Bognors nodded, a little apprehensive now.

'And how was it?' Wartnaby might have been enquiring about the weather or trying to determine whether someone would like one lump or two.

Bognor countered. 'All right,' he said. 'Hardly one of the gastronomic treats of a lifetime.'

Wartnaby smiled. 'Great eaters of roast beef, the Artisans,

though for my part I believe it does harm to their wit.'

Bognor looked blank.

'Is there no respect of place, persons, nor time, in you?' asked Monica.

Bognor realised he was caught up in what threatened to become a private mastermind contest on Shakespearean comedy. What on earth was the police force coming to?

'Had you any previous experience of the Artisans, Mr Bognor?'

Simon had already decided that this was one of those rare policemen with whom he probably ought to be on Christian-name terms.

'Simon,' he said.

'Osbert,' said Wartnaby.

'Golly,' said Monica.

Wartnaby looked at her sharply. 'Osbert Sitwell, Osbert Lancaster, not to mention Osbert Burdett who wrote a life of Carlyle and of Browning. It's a perfectly sensible name, even if unusual. Besides which it's really only one among the many Berts as in Al, Cuth or even Eg or Ethel. As it happens, practically everyone in the world calls me Bert. People are depressingly conventional about Christian names.'

Now, at last, he did take a sip of coffee. His lip puckered. 'Never drink coffee at the Talbot,' he said. 'Or any of the Jolly Trenchermen. You'd think Puce would do something about it. I'm a Kibo Chagga man myself, though I had a first-rate Costa Rican Tarrazu the other day. Anyway, "Bert" will do fine, but for God's sake not "Oz", much less "Ozzy".'

'I knew a Canadian once who called me "Si",' said Bognor. He winced to recall it.

Osbert Wartnaby pushed his cup away and leaned forward. 'I'm going to need your help,' he said.

This was the most surprising thing this surprising police-man had said thus far. The police rarely wanted Bognor's support. They almost invariably resented his very presence. Any effort to become involved in actually solving a mystery was obstructed, often physically. Wartnaby's initiative, therefore, was as unexpected as it was welcome.

'Help,' repeated Bognor, beginning to butter another slice of toast in celebration.

'Yes.' Wartnaby eyed the toast-buttering. He was much of an age with Bognor, but trim and spry. The glance carried an element of censorious superiority. 'I need your help.'

'Of course,' said Bognor, avoiding his wife's eye. 'How can I assist you?'

'How much do you know about the Artisans?'

'Not much more than what Reg Brackett and Harold Fothergill told me.'

'You'd already met Brackett?'

'The day before yesterday. He was my second port of call. Fothergill said I ought to start with him if I wanted to know what made Scarpington tick.'

'So what did they tell you about the Artisans?' Wartnaby took a stainless steel Parker from an inside pocket. 'You don't mind if I take a note.' He produced a leather pad about three inches by six. It was more of a statement than a question. Even if Bognor had objected, Wartnaby was going to make notes.

'To paraphrase,' said Bognor. 'That it was an association of local trade, business and professional people given to good works and conviviality. Rather like Rotary only grander and with a history that went back to the seventeenth century.'

'Correct up to a point,' said Wartnaby. 'You'll discover that both Moulton and Bragg, the brewers, and Sinclair, the invalid carriage people, can trace their origins back to around the Restoration.'

'Seventeenth-century invalid carriages?' said Monica. 'Surely not?'

'There's some dispute,' said Wartnaby, 'about whether Sinclair's started out in sedan chairs or wooden legs. At all events they've always been in what one might loosely term transport for the disabled. And both of them were founder members of the Artisans. The earliest charters date from 1690-odd.'

'So they're Orange.' This from Bognor, who still remembered the dates of the kings and queens of England despite the amnesia creeping up on his middle age. 1688. Glorious Revolution. William and Mary.

'Very Orange.' Wartnaby spoke with feeling.

'You don't sound over enthusiastic,' said Bognor.

'No. And it's why I need your help.' Wartnaby paused. 'This is still a very Orange town,' he said. 'I know because I've lived here all my life. It's not a very comfortable community for a Jewish Roman Catholic. Which is what I am. Lapsed on both sides of the family, but that doesn't make any odds. Scarpington must be the most extreme Protestant town outside Ulster and the most extreme Protestantism is in the Artisans.'

Neither Bognor said anything. There was nothing much to say. All around them was the comfortable evidence of the English middle class at breakfast on the hoof. Middling to posh hotel; middling to dull provincial city; bacon, eggs; Baxter's and Cooper's marmalades in the usual minipots; and the *Daily Telegraph*. The smarter sort of commercial traveller was dotted all over the dining-room, each one in solitary embarrassment, feigning assurance and man-of-the-worldliness. The odd woman out was a very odd woman out, except for the black-and-white waitresses in their pinnies. It could, apart from the muesli and the yoghurt laid out on a central buffet table, have been any business breakfast in Britain from around the turn of the century on. It was axiomatic that beneath the pastoral bucolic charm of the English countryside there lurked any number of hidden menaces. But wasn't it just as true of this outwardly prim prosperity? What hidden seethings bubbled behind those morning papers? What lusts and envies disturbed the heartbeat under those clean white drip-dry shirts? Crime and the commercial traveller: discuss.

'Wartnaby's not a very Jewish name,' said Bognor.

'Osbert's mother, dummy!' Monica could be so gratuitously disparaging.

'My mother was from Estonia. My father was merchant navy. He helped her escape. Very romantic. And then they ended up here.' His eyes traversed the dining-room of the

Talbot Hotel and moved upwards to the chandelier. They spoke volumes.

'I went to the King's School. That was my first brush with the Scarpington Establishment. It was stiff with Sinclairs and Bracketts and Moultons and Festings. All died-in-the-wool Proddies. There was a lot of bullying at the King's School and a great deal of it was ritualised and institutionalised. It was an exceedingly dim place academically. Whenever anybody got into Oxford or Cambridge they lit a bonfire. It only happened twice the whole time I was there. Puce and Nigel Festing.'

'Puce?' said Bognor. 'You mean Seymour Puce?'

'Absolutely,' said Wartnaby. 'He was the school bully. Only, as I said, it was legal. He was head of school, captain of the Fifteen, RSM of the Corps. You name it. He beat like fury. We called him "Shagger" Puce. Something to do with sheep.'

For a moment it looked as if he might be about to take a sip of the undrinkable coffee. Instead he asked a passing waitress if he might have a glass of water. She looked as if he had asked for a double Negroni, heavy on the gin, but she agreed to fetch it. Wartnaby was obviously, in his understated fashion, a man accustomed to having his way.

'And you,' said Monica. 'You didn't go to university.'

'My father ran a milk bar called the Coconut Grove in the Ackroyd Road. Early one morning he was knocked down by a hit-and-run driver on his way to work. They never found the killer. My mother took an overdose a fortnight later. I was just sixteen. Only child.'

Monica and her husband exchanged glances. They weren't entirely sure where, if anywhere, this was all leading. It was an upsetting tale and intimate. They had only known Wartnaby a few minutes and now they had his life story.

'So what did you do?' Wartnaby was obviously going to tell them, but Bognor felt he needed a mild prompt. His glass of water arrived and was plonked down on the table with scant ceremony. He drank.

'I ran away,' he said. 'Signed on as a cabin boy on a

29

Dutch freighter at Avonmouth. Worked as a croupier in Macao for a year; in a logging camp at Gold River on Vancouver island for another; did a summer season on the ground staff at the Kensington Oval in Barbados and then got homesick and came back here. Married a local girl and joined the police. Been here ever since.'

Very long pause. The Bognors were strapped for words.

'The Artisans,' said Bognor at last. 'You were asking about the Artisans.'

DCI Wartnaby smiled. 'Sorry,' he said, 'but my life history is sort of relevant. I'm a Scarpington man through and through, but when it comes to the power base I'm an outsider. As I said, Jewish and Catholic. That rules me out on two counts. And there are others. At school I was what used to be called a "bolshie". Questioned authority, no good at rugger, cheeky sod.'

'Didn't like Puce,' ventured Bognor.

'Didn't like Puce,' repeated Wartnaby thoughtfully. A cloud seemed to pass briefly across his face as if some unexpected memory had suddenly re-emerged. For a moment the Bognors sensed that he was going to share it with them, but he checked himself. Perhaps too painful, perhaps too intimate.

'The point is,' he said in a voice that was now more purposeful and brisk as if the earlier revelations were just a necessary overture to the main work, 'the point is that as far as the Artisans are concerned I am distinctly *persona non grata*. Now I am reasonably sure that when the post-mortem comes through it is going to show that Reg Brackett had a heart attack. And I dare say his GP will come through with some corroborating evidence about a history of stress and high blood pressure and I'm sure Muriel Brackett will confirm that he had been under a lot of strain and that he was particularly hyped up about his big night and the after-dinner speech. And in the normal course of events the whole thing would be sloughed off as one of life's little tragedies. Poor old Reg. Dreadful thing. Should have watched his diet, cut the fags, laid off the booze. Blah blah.'

'But you don't think that's what happened?'

'No.'

'Any reason?'

Wartnaby thought for a moment.

'King's Scarpington,' he said, 'was not just a dim school with a bad academic record and a problem of violence. It was a deeply corrupt school. And the heart of the corruption was something called Upper Tucker. It was a sort of semi-secret society for the smart set – a pastiche of something called Pop at Eton. The whole place was a sort of parody of a proper public school. The headmaster and the rest of the staff counted for nothing. It was a boy-run school and it was run from Upper Tucker.

'Now normally, as you know, success at school doesn't necessarily mean success in after-life. It's often the reverse. But in Scarpington the lines run directly out of the King's School and on through adulthood to the grave. Modern Scarpington, Mr Bognor, is as deeply corrupt as the school was. And is. And the centre of it is the Artisans.'

'Are you sure?' Bognor was beginning to think that Wartnaby was a bit of a nut-case. Whatever it was that Puce had done to him all those years ago could have turned his mind. Joining the local police was obviously done to get even. The awfulness had languished in a diseased mind for years and now he saw the chance of revenge. The vendetta had reached maturity; the kettle had come to the boil.

'I promise you,' said the Chief Inspector, slowly, 'that the Artisans would make the most sinister Masonic Lodge in the world look like the Women's Institute. They have the whole of Scarpington in their pocket one way and another. My own Chief Constable included.'

'And,' said Bognor, 'not to put too fine a point on it, you think that they bumped off their own President in the middle of his after-dinner speech? That's a pretty rum thing to do, isn't it? I mean, they may be corrupt but there's usually a logic to corruption.'

'You're right.' Wartnaby frowned. 'In logic. But my sense is that logic doesn't necessarily enter into this. Or put it

31

another way – there is a logic at work but it's perverted. I don't think, for instance, that it's beyond the bounds of possibility that Brackett was killed as a warning.'

'Pour encourager les autres.' Bognor remembered Byng.

'It's only an idea.' He looked morose. 'To be absolutely frank, I can't put my finger on anything, but I know it stinks and the more it stinks the more squeaky clean they make it look. Laundry's appropriate. That's just what they've been doing for years. Taking in each other's dirty linen. Brackett did it literally and everyone else did it metaphorically. And they know I know. I'm sure of it. And it's my belief that this time they've overstepped the mark.'

'How long have you suspected them?'

'In general terms, as long as I can remember.' Wartnaby obviously sensed their scepticism. 'I can see,' he said, 'you think I'm paranoid. Yes, if you like, I've had a bee in my bonnet about Puce and his friends since I was a child. Yes, I'm deeply suspicious about my father's death. Yes, I joined the police because I saw myself as a crusader and I wanted to clean the town up. Guilty on all counts. I concede I could be wrong. But my point is that I'll never have the chance of finding out unless I have help. The Artisans are a closed book as far as I'm concerned. No one will even begin to talk. My colleagues – most of them – are either involved with them or too frightened to take them on. You, on the other hand, are white, Anglo-Saxon Protestant, non-Artisan, non-Scarpington, and non-police. You're no threat to them. To you they will talk. All I ask is that you interview them all as soon as possible and let me know what they say.'

'That sounds a bit one-sided,' said Bognor. 'What, if you'll excuse the crudity, is in it for me?'

'I'll guide your feet into the way of peace.' Wartnaby was doodling as he talked. Peacock feathers seemed to be the dominant refrain which would have meant something to a graphologist, Tarot-freak, end-of-pier gypsy lady or similar, but not a lot to Bognor, though Monica, being superstitious, would not have them in the house. Something to do with the evil eye. 'I,' continued Wartnaby, 'can save you weeks of labour. My knowledge might not stand up in a court of law but it's the real thing. Hearsay, gossip, intuition and a life-time's experience. All yours in return for up-to-the-minute, on-the-record, first-hand, viva-voce gen.'

'You're on,' said Bognor, with a sudden exuberance which took them all, most of all himself, by surprise. 'When do we start?'

'In skating over thin ice,' said Wartnaby, 'our safety is in our speed. My Jewish grandmother always said it was best to start yesterday what one didn't have to start tomorrow. Or words to that effect.'

'I'm happy to be guided by your granny,' said Bognor. 'Who's first on the list?'

'I'd begin with Freddie.'

'The barman.'

'The same.'

'But surely he's not an "Artisan" except in a literal sense?'

'He knows more about the Artisans than most Artisans,' said Wartnaby, 'and more about Scarpington than almost anyone in town. My hunch is that he'd quite enjoy talking to you. Particularly if the Board of Trade budget extends to a modest bribe. A tenner should do the trick.'

CHAPTER THREE

Face to Face with the Pilot

Bartending is primarily a nocturnal activity. Bognor had done his fair share of daytime drinking over the years and spent long hours in the company of dangerous daytime drunks. He could recall an afternoon of double g and ts with an elderly actor at the Wig and Pen and inordinate quantities of Scotch with a load of Fleet Street hacks in a very dark room in Soho run by a noisy woman, famed for her rudeness. But these, at least to his way of thinking, were aberrations. Despite changes in the licensing laws his reaction to being asked if he would take some alcohol was the same as most Englishmen's. He looked at his watch. If it was after six and the sun was therefore 'over the yard-arm' it was acceptable to imbibe. If not, not. Some exception was permissible at lunchtime but not, these days, a lot.

This somewhat old-fashioned, not to say pedestrian, interpretation was more prevalent in Scarpington than in London. Of course there was some daytime drinking. On the days of Scarpington Thursday's home games when the visiting fans were escorted down the High Street by a handful of Scarpington's finest, mounted on horses which looked suspiciously as if they should be hauling milk floats, an element of lager-louting could be found. This did not, however, penetrate the Talbot or Freddie's bar. On Market Day – Thursday, which was, incidentally, the reason for the football team's curious name – farmers from the outlying countryside had been known to take a drop or two, but only the richest and grandest hung out in Freddie's. A few, a very few, Artisans occasionally dropped in for a snifter before lunch, especially if they were having the meal in the Talbot's stately, over-priced dining-room which was still serving a style of cooking that was little more than an appalling folk memory for people who lived elsewhere in Britain.

But, generally speaking, Freddie's bar was pretty quiet until evening.

It followed from this that during the day Freddie himself was pretty quiet too. In the evening he could be seen to be doing a fair amount of what one might call work, occasionally even shaking the odd cocktail. But before sixish he left practically everything to one or other of his assistants. These were invariably pretty if acne'd young men who were always called Gavin or Terry and left after not more than six months. This was the result of long hours, low wages and, it was sometimes alleged, sexual harassment by Freddie. Indeed Wartnaby suggested that on one occasion Freddie had actually been caught 'cottaging' by the Scarpington vice squad which spent much time hanging around public lavatories hoping to trap an invariably pathetic queen or two by acting as *agents provocateurs*. Wartnaby was of the opinion that Puce had somehow caused the charges to be dropped, thus giving the MP an unshakeable hold over the barman.

Freddie's routine was to arrive shortly before the bar opened at 11.30. He would then fix a Virgin Mary or, if the mood took him, a Bloody, mixed to an ancient recipe which went very heavy on the tabasco. He would then sit on a high stool in one corner of his bar and read grimly through the racing pages of the *Daily Express* and the *Sporting Life* before telephoning Sparks, the bookmaker, to place his day's bets. Sparks, incidentally, was not an Artisan – bookmaking being essentially a non-Artisan activity.

With an hour or so to kill before the shutters would be pulled aside at the St Moritz, Bognor and his spouse took a rather lethargic constitutional along the banks of the not tremendously picturesque River Sludgelode – Anglo-Saxon for sludgy ditch or small water course, Monica explained helpfully. The towpath ran alongside Moulton and Bragg's brewery and Sinclair's invalid carriage works and out to Sludgelode Fen where the King's School Playing Fields were. The path was littered with the traditional mess of fag ends, dog turds and used condoms and as the day was dank the Bognors returned to the hotel damp and dispirited.

'I'm going to take a peek at the Cathedral,' said Monica, 'to see if it'll cheer me up. If it doesn't I think I'm going back to London.'

Bognor paled.

'For God's sake don't do that,' he said, genuinely alarmed. 'You can't leave me here all alone.'

'You wouldn't be alone,' said Monica. 'You'd have nice Inspector Wartnaby and all those perfectly charming Artisans.'

'That's what I mean,' said Bognor.

When he finally entered the St Moritz it was just noon and Freddie was just where Wartnaby had said he would be, doing just as had been predicted. The *Sporting Life* was folded in front of him and the barman, much-chewed yellow pencil poised above the card for this afternoon's racing at Chepstow, was studying form.

'Morning!' said Bognor with a cheeriness he was far from feeling.

One of the Gavins said 'Morning, sir' with tolerable brightness and Bognor toyed with joining Freddie in a Virgin Mary before deciding on a half pint of Old Parsnip. He felt there was something hypocritical about soft drinking in licensed premises. And a half pint wouldn't do a lot of harm. Besides, a half of Old Parsnip was good cover. It was what Freddie would expect from a Board of Trade special investigator engaged in ordinary, routine run-of-the-mill Board of Trade special investigations. If he had been asking serious questions about a murder he would have had a Perrier with ice and lemon. No question.

'First rate stuff, this Parsnip,' he said, in an effort to break the ice and lead into serious questioning with some genial banter. Bognor reckoned his line in genial banter was almost of professional standard. Indeed when it came to genial banter he thought of himself as international class. Give him a microphone and a clutch of celebrities and he could match Terry Wogan or Johnny Carson any day of the week. He sat down on the high-backed bar stool nearest Freddie and gave a hitch to his brown corduroy trousers, newly purchased because he thought they would be just the thing for Scarpington. He was also wearing his vivid pink and purple Arkwright and Blennerhasset Society tie. The A and B had been his college debating society. That and a check shirt with a Harris tweed jacket completed a picture which, in his humble opinion, was just the ticket for middle England. It wouldn't do to seem too smart or to have tried too hard, but one's clothing should be tolerably well made and neutral in tone. Beige, he felt, was the colour most appropriate to middle England. Beige with a loud, striped, meaningful tie. He liked to think that he would have passed without comment in the masters' Common Room at the King's School.

However, in response to his 'First rate stuff, this Parsnip', the barman said not a word.

Bognor sipped the beer, which was indeed excellent, and gazed at the stuffed ferret which reposed on the shelf behind Freddie among the bottles of esoteric whiskies.

'That a ferret?' he bantered.

Gavin, polishing a glass, seemed not to hear. Freddie, engrossed in his horses, did not react either.

Bognor sighed. Perhaps, after all, the full frontal approach would be best. This subtle conversational opening was going nowhere. There was no one else in the bar. The only sound came from the traditional St Moritz cuckoo clock. Why faff around discussing beer and ferrets when they might be getting down to brass tacks?

He tried again.

'Freddie,' he said, regretting as he did that he did not

know Freddie's surname. A touch of formality would not, he felt, have come amiss.

'Mr Bognor.' Freddie raised his eyes to engage Bognor's. They were pink and rheumy and they twitched. His hand, the one with the pencil in it, twitched too. He did not seem to be in good order. It occurred to Bognor to wonder if, apart from a look of alcoholic dereliction, he also had an appearance of criminal guilt. After all, if Brackett had been murdered, Freddie was in a good position to administer a lethal dose of something liquid.

'I wonder if I might have a word?' Bognor grinned with an affability he did not feel.

Freddie looked inscrutable and not encouraging. Eventually he said, 'Feel free.'

'I'm here to do a survey for my employers, the Board of Trade,' said Bognor.

'I know,' said Freddie. He took a translucent cocktail onion from an ash tray, peered at it and then popped it into his mouth. His teeth had the wondrous regularity and sheen which only the National Health can give.

'A sort of general view of what makes the town tick. From a commercial and business point of view.'

Freddie looked at him in much the same way as he had looked at the onion. This time he said nothing, but nodded.

Bognor ploughed on regardless. 'I'm told you've been here for more than thirty years. You must have been able to form a pretty authoritative view after all that time.'

Freddie seemed to be cogitating. Bognor could almost hear the wheels and cogs crunching grey matter about inside that pink, twitching, decayed apology for a head. Bognor wasn't liking Freddie. He decided to show Freddie his visiting card which would also give him a good view of the inside of his wallet, which happened to be well stuffed with paper money. Freddie perked up at this.

'What's it worth?'

'Twenty quid.'

'What do you want to know?' Freddie took the two

ten-pound notes. Gavin watched surreptitiously. 'I'm not giving away any secrets,' continued the bartender. 'More than my job's worth.' Bognor guessed this was probably true. With Sir Seymour Puce as the top banana he could imagine a word out of turn leading to a no-questions-asked instant dismissal. Even after thirty years' service.

'Well, for a start,' said Bognor, 'who do you think I should talk to if I really want to find out how the town works?'

'Works?' Freddie swirled a Jolly Trencherman swizzle stick round his drink. 'Depends what you mean by works.'

Oh God, Bognor thought to himself. It was going to be one of those interviews. But the barman was beginning to slip into gear. 'I'll be honest with you, Mr Bognor,' he said, with a leer which invalidated the suggestion immediately. 'My experience is that there are two sorts of situation in life. One is when everything is exactly what it seems. The other is when it's not.'

Bognor blasphemed inwardly again. He supposed this sort of philosophy was a hazard of talking to barmen, but it didn't make it any the less tiresome. He nodded agreement, catching, as he did, a waft of fetid breath stale with pickle and alcohol and cheap cigarette.

'Now, take Scarpington.'

Bognor nodded again, eyes beginning to glaze. Dammit, he must concentrate. This was supposed to be the most knowledgeable man in Scarpington.

'When I first came here,' said Freddie, 'the d'eath-Stranglefields owned the whole of the city and much else besides.'

'The d'eath-Stranglefields being the Earl's family?' Bognor had done a little homework.

'Only that was the old Earl, the present Earl's father. He was a real gentleman.'

Bognor had a dim recollection of an unreconstructed backwoodsman in an I Zingari tie who descended on the House of Lords once a year to make a choleric intervention on behalf of the blood sport lobby. People like Freddie always thought people like that were 'real gentlemen'.

'Then,' continued Freddie, 'when the old Earl died there were the death duties.'

He smacked his lips.

'That was a bad time for the family. There was talk of them selling up and moving to South Africa. The Dowager Countess, that's the present Earl's mother, gone now, poor soul, was in a dreadful rage, I recall. Blamed it all on the socialists and Mr Butler who she said was a socialist in disguise. They had to sell off a lot of the property. They say some of the diamonds went too and that what the Countess wears now are just paste.'

'Who did they sell to?' Bognor had a hunch he knew the answer already.

'A lot of it went to old man Puce. Ivan his name was. Worked his way up from nothing. Don't ask me how he did it, but he was a clever lad. They say he was a racketeer during the war but I don't set too much store by that. He wouldn't have been the only one.'

'Not a gentleman?' Bognor could not resist the dig but the barman was not into sarcasm.

'Not even one of nature's,' he said. 'Not like Sir Seymour. But then if you want to get on in the world you have to cut a few corners. No use playing to the Queensberry rules when the other fellow's headbutting and punching you in the kidneys. Like the man says, "you've got to get your retaliation in first". Munitions, nylons, booze, all the black market stuff. Nobody knows the whole truth but by the time the old Earl pegged out the Puces were worth a lot of money. Property, car parks, some of it down in London, they say.'

'Who's "they"?' Bognor wanted to know.

Freddie smiled his flashing dentures in a contemptuous grimace. 'You won't catch me revealing my sources, Mr Bognor,' he said. 'In any event, when I came on the scene in the fifties Ivan Puce was a big man in Scarpington. Rolls-Royce, big Havanas, a string of blondes with strings of pearls, strings of racehorses, an estate on the banks of the Sludgelode. You get the picture?'

Bognor got the picture.

'Gresham's Law,' he said.

Freddie frowned.

'Bad money drives out good.'

'There was nothing bad about the Puce money. It was real. It was the Earl's cheques that bounced; the Earl's creditors who had to wait to get paid.'

'Well, then,' Bognor wanted to seem conciliatory, 'new money drives out old. Not quite the same thing.'

'Not at all the same thing, with respect.'

This was obviously a Thatcherite barman. But the story he told was a story of the times. The Rise and Fall of the Gentry. Each century had its *nouveaux riches* and its decaying aristocracy. But it was Bognor's view that the newest generation of parvenus were spivvier than most while the aristocrats they displaced were more than usually dilapidated. But maybe every generation thought like that.

'And now?' asked Bognor. 'What's the state of play now?'

Freddie seemed to hesitate, then took a plunge. 'Sir Seymour is the MP; he's Chairman of Puce Investments; and Puce Developments; and Puce Properties; and the Jolly Trencherman chain of hotels; and Scarpington Thursday. I'm not giving anything away when I tell you that.' This last was defensive. He really did not want to be accused of telling tales. 'And Lord Scarpington resides in Scarpington Castle, plays a bit of golf, sits on some boards and some benches. He's not the man his father was. And as for the Countess . . .'

Bognor had noticed Diana, Countess of Scarpington, at the dinner last night. She was the second Countess and was the modern equivalent of a chorus girl. In other words, she had been in some sort of public relations. Upmarket PR as they called it. She was thirty-fiveish, stylish and, last night at least, more than a little tipsy. High cheekbones, eyes like feline soup-bowls and an over-generous mouth and cleavage. Trouble.

'And as for the Countess . . . ?'

Freddie wasn't saying. The sub-text was there for the

most illiterate to decipher, but Freddie wasn't spelling it out. Not for twenty quid. Bognor thought about it for a while and then decided not to press the point. It was almost certainly not relevant.

'So where do the Artisans fit into all this?'

The barman smirked.

'If I were to mix us both a Scarpington Special,' he said, 'would you imbibe with me?'

'A Scarpington Special?' Bognor did not know this drink.

'Same as a Saigon Special, only with a squirt of peach bitters and half a jigger of Old Parsnip to give it a little local colour. Not unlike a Jerusalem Between-the-Sheets.'

Bognor had to admit that he was not familiar with a Jerusalem Between-the-Sheets either.

Suddenly the barman's eyes sparkled and he slid off the stool and seemed to shed twenty or more years. 'Two Scarpington Specials coming up,' he said with a flick of the hips and wrist which caused Gavin to pause from his washing-up and suck his teeth.

'Cognac. Only the best. VSOP. Hine for Her Majesty's sake. One pony. Dry gin. Gordon's, one half a pony. Cointreau, the same. Lemon juice, one half teaspoon. Two teaspoons of egg white. And the merest soupçon of peach bitters. With the half jigger of Parsnip to finish. Crushed ice.' He reached for a battered cocktail shaker which sat alongside the stuffed ferret. He poured and sieved and crushed and shook and was galvanised into something quite unrecognisable. It all took longer to perform than recite but before too terribly long two tall-stemmed cocktail glasses were on the bar full of frothing icy Special. Bognor sipped and felt the back of his head take a pace backwards.

'Wow,' he said. 'Where did you learn that?'

'It dates,' said Freddie, 'back to the SS *Resolute* in the year 1925 somewhere between Saigon and Pak Nam. Oh Christ, I forgot the cherry.' Whereupon he found two, stuck them on sticks and plonked them into the drinks.

'Yes, but . . .' Bognor had not had a proper answer.

'I worked for Roy Aciatore at Antoine's in New Orleans

after I was demobbed,' answered Freddie. 'He taught me the Sazarac. I could do you a September Morn like they shook at the Ingleterre in Havana before Castro was conceived. Or a Kelly Shamrock Special or a Shanghai Buck or an Anejo Candido or a Wilson's South Camp Road or a Rangoon Star Ruby or a Sunday Vespers or a Vladivostock Virgin or a White Rat which has a jigger of absinthe and a half pony of anis del mono. Or Farewell to Hemingway which is a kirsch collins with a spiral of green lime. Ye Gods, but doesn't it make you weep.'

Bognor sort of agreed. In fact he was transfixed. The little barman was transformed. In fact, briefly, he was poetry in potion.

Bognor took another short draught of the exotic drink and began to worry about the remainder of his day.

'Amazing!' he said, and then a cloud of doubt and apprehension no larger than a man's fist passed briefly before his eyes. He saw Freddie squirt the remainder of his peach bitters into the little barman's sink and he watched him put a small, water-pistol-like object back into his trouser pocket.

'I say,' he said, 'now what's that?'

And just as suddenly the mood was changed and they were back from Havana and Saigon and New Orleans and the ghosts of Papa Hemingway and Roy Aciatore and they were home where they both belonged in the tarted-up bar of a three-star hotel in middle England where a man had died not far away the night before telling one of the oldest jokes in Britain. And Bognor said again, 'What's that?'

And the barman coughed and drank and said, 'It was a present from Hubert on the old *Queen Mary*. A barman's friend. Your old quill-top bottle stopper which none of us would have been without in the good old days before Real Ale and Wine Bars when cocktails were cocktails.'

'Fascinating,' said Bognor. 'Could I have a look?'

'I'm sorry, no,' said Freddie and the fist in front of Bognor's eyes grew a little larger. 'It's just, well, personal, you know, like.'

So Bognor changed the subject and asked him what a world-class cocktailer like him was doing in a dump like this and Freddie shrugged and said that life was a funny thing.

'So,' Bognor returned to the matter in hand. 'Tell me about the Artisans.'

And up to a point and in a manner of speaking he did. But the mood had changed beyond repair. Freddie had seemed on the verge of euphoric disclosure, a return to the days of wine and roses when he was young and fancy-free in New Orleans or on the High Seas. For a few moments, faced with the choice between telling Bognor about the world as it seemed and the world as it was, he had appeared to be on the verge of expounding the second. In the end he gave him the first. He did not lie but he was economical with the truth. He also made a second Scarpington Special, but without the sudden access of nostalgic enthusiasm it was not as good as it seemed. And Bognor noticed that this time he did not use his barman's friend – the little quill-topped bottle stopper for squirting infinitesimal quantities of bitters. This time Bognor did not mention it.

The information was all right as far as it went. Bognor already knew that, according to the original charter of the Artisans, drawn up in the reign of bad King John and last seriously amended in the reign of Edward VII, there could only be thirty-nine full Artisans, though there could be any number of Associates. These Associates, like the more notorious legion of Associate Members of the Marylebone Cricket Club, constituted a form of waiting list, enjoyed minimal privileges and contributed liberally to the Artisans' Coffers. There was a Council of Thirteen, a President, a Vice-President, a Grand Patron (the Earl), a Chaplain (the Bishop), and a Treasurer (Puce). The Traditional Office of Sconce Bearer was in perpetual abeyance and the Visitor was Hiis Majesty the King of Norway who had never attended any Artisan Functions nor ever replied to any Artisan correspondence. The Council consisted of President Brackett, Vice-President Brown of Brown's Dairy (who now succeeded the deceased just as Dan Quayle would succeed George Bush in the event of any similar unpleasantness) and Puce. The remaining Council members were, in order of seniority: Fothergill of the *Times*, Sinclair the invalid carriage maker, Festing the solicitor, Moulton the Brewer, Green, the builder's merchant, and Doctor Dick. The Earl, the Bishop and the King were Honorary Members but did not attend Council meetings. And the thirteenth was a Queen's Counsel called Benger who was in his ninety-third year and was confined to a home for distressed gentlefolk where he languished under the impression that he was the Master of the Rolls. He was, needless to say, not allowed out.

Because Freddie, even allowing for the second Special, was being the acme of discretion, Bognor did not glean a great deal from the biographical sketches he provided. On the other hand, by listening carefully to what was left unsaid and by putting the occasional two and two together to make five he began to build a dossier. Brackett appeared to be a nice little man with no business sense. Remembering Fothergill's opinion to the contrary, Bognor pressed the point.

'Mr Fothergill and Mr Brackett had a falling out over golf some years back,' said Freddie. 'I'm not a golfing man myself. Someone moved a ball. Or didn't move a ball. There was a lot of feeling.'

'And what about Mrs Fothergill?' Bognor continued. 'She seemed to have quite a soft spot for Mr Brackett.'

For a second Bognor sensed a confusion in Freddie which might or might not have hinted at something irregular, but if so he recovered swiftly. 'I believe,' he said, 'they partnered each other at, er, bridge, from time to time.' Was it Bognor's imagination or did Freddie hesitate before the word 'bridge'? If so it was marginal and the barman's speech appeared to be hesitant at the best of times.

'Does Mr Fothergill play bridge?'

Again Bognor sensed a shiftiness.

'Not as far as I know. A lot of the bridge goes on in the afternoons and Mr Fothergill tends to be busy during the day. Always says he's got a newspaper to bring out.'

Bognor scribbled 'Fothergill self-important' in his notebook and added 'Reg Brackett=Edna Fothergill?'

'Bridge popular in Artisan circles, Freddie?' he asked.

'More so among the Artisans' wives, Mr Bognor.' Freddie seemed to be daring him to make more of this. Bognor guessed that bridge and good works would be significant if not universal diversions among the wives of middle England. He must ask Monica for an opinion.

'But Mr Brackett could sometimes slip away for an afternoon's bridge.'

'Mr Brackett always used to say the laundry ran itself,' said Freddie. 'God rest his soul.'

'Did he?' Bognor did not make a further jotting since this was merely corroboration of a belief universally held. Bracketts Laundry and Dry Cleaning Services had obviously been allowed to run itself for some time and in doing so had run itself virtually into the ground. If Brackett had been killed, as Osbert Wartnaby seemed to think, then could this fecklessness provide a motive? For the moment Bognor did not quite see how, but it might be worth pursuing.

'So who plays bridge and where?' asked Bognor, changing tack.

'I couldn't say for absolute certain,' said Freddie. He really didn't seem to enjoy the questions about bridge. 'Dr Dick's very keen, and Mrs Moulton and Mrs Festing and Mrs Sinclair come to that.'

'But not their husbands?'

'Not nearly as keen.'

A group of rather shapeless dark suits had entered the St Moritz bar and been served with sweet sherry and white wine spritzers by Gavin. Bognor glanced across at them and, turning back to Freddie, raised an interlocutory eyebrow. 'Regulars?'

'Out of town, Mr Bognor. Representatives of some description, I should imagine.'

'Perhaps they're from Mr Clean or Bleach'n'Starch,' said Bognor, 'come like vultures to pick over the corpse.'

Freddie gave Bognor an extremely old-fashioned look at this.

'Do you do the stock market as well as the gee-gees?' Bognor had had another of his impulses.

'I prefer to stick with animals, Mr Bognor. I've always found them more reliable than humans.'

Very meaningful, thought Bognor. Freddie was a mis-anthropic old buzzard. He guessed barmen always were. You could hardly spend a lifetime watching people get drunk and listening to their inebriated catalogue of woes and misfortunes without developing a jaundiced view of the human race. Perhaps it was a rule that everyone in the service industry despised their clients. It was certainly true of waiters and said to be true of tarts. Bognor considered the barman's heart of gold as illusory as the prostitute's. His only experience of the latter had been professional. 'Immoral earnings' occasionally came within his ambit.

'Anything else I should know about the Artisans, Freddie? They do seem to represent the absolute heart of the Scarpington community.'

'Couldn't have put it better myself,' said Freddie. He seemed relieved to sense that the interview was coming to an end. 'Heart and soul.'

'I don't suppose there's any chance of my sitting in on any of their meetings?' he said, as a final question.

Freddie shook his head. 'Gracious, no. The annual dinner's the only time guests are allowed, Mr Bognor. Otherwise they're very private.'

' "Private" Freddie, or "Secret"?'

Bognor, through what, he suddenly realised, was a fog of exotic alcohol, felt that this was a fine distinction, so he repeated it slowly in the hope of nonplussing his inter-viewee, who, he reckoned, should be almost as drunk as he was himself. After all, he, Bognor, was only a half of Parsnip ahead.

'Private or Secret?'

'Comes to the same thing,' said Freddie, not, seemingly, in the least nonplussed.

'I'm not so sure about that,' said Bognor. 'I mean, they could get up to all sorts of nonsense in what you call "private". Like the freemasons. Mad oaths and rituals.'

'Oh, there's an Artisan oath,' said Freddie. 'Not that I know what it says. I do know the penalty for breaking it, though.'

'Which is?' Bognor, despite having taken drink, was pretty certain what the answer was going to be, but even so, and even allowing for the fact that in this day and age it would hardly be invoked, it still chilled him when it came.

'Death,' said the barman.

CHAPTER FOUR

An English Countess goes upon the Stage

Monica was not in their room, but there was a note stuck to the frame of the dressing-table mirror. 'Cathedral is parish church in all but name. Hideous banners woven by Townswomen's Guild. V. Bored Scarpington. Have gone to flicks for matinee. See you teatime. Love, M.'

Oh, well. Bognor kicked off his shoes, lay down on the bed, and consulted the room service menu. It was all chargeable to boring old Parkinson. He fancied a cheeseburger. It wouldn't put on any weight if he left the chips. The cocktails had made him thirsty as well as wobbly. He wondered if he should have something soft but the idea was not appealing. Perhaps he should compromise and have a low cal lager. Maybe they did a low cal Parsnip. He would ask. He turned to his notes and squinted at them. Difficult to decipher. Never mind, he prided himself on his photographic, well, near photographic memory. Besides, the barman would be there again this evening and tomorrow and the next day. He could always ask again. Damn and blast, he hadn't pursued the question about where the Artisan wives played their bridge. He had been deflected by the untimely arrival of the people in the suits with their ridiculous white wine spritzers. Perhaps he should have a white wine spritzer with his cheeseburger. No, it didn't go, it really didn't. Maybe a steak. Parkinson would be bound to query it, he'd better not. Besides if Monica had eaten on the hoof she'd be ratty about it and she sounded ratty enough already.

He dialled seven.

'Marketing,' said a nasal male Scarpingtonian voice.

'I wanted room service.'

'Well, you've come through to marketing.'

'Can you put me back to the switchboard?'

'Just replace your receiver and dial "7" for room service. This is marketing.' There was a click and drone as the man in marketing replaced his receiver.

Bognor swore very loudly and dialled "7" again.

This time a female Scarpington voice answered, flat and bored and none too bright.

'Yes,' it said.

'Is that room service?'

Pause. Then, 'Room Service.'

'Do you do low cal Old Parsnip?'

There was another click and drone as this receiver was also replaced. Bognor wondered whether he might risk an amble down to the dining-room but decided to make one last effort. This time he established a genuine two-way communication with what sounded like a Spanish person who admitted to being room service but said all burgers were off. Bognor asked if he could have steak. Steak was on. There was no low cal Parsnip so he ordered a pint of the real thing. Frankly it was too much hassle to do otherwise. He would go easy later on.

He returned to his notes. What next, he wondered. The obvious thing was to work through the Artisan Committee. At least that seemed the most obvious thing. It certainly fitted in with his brief from Parkinson and was what he had been intending to do when poor Brackett kicked the bucket. Where to start, though? The top seemed the best idea. The Earl was presumably still in town, or, at least, just outside at Scarpington Castle, rumoured to be the least comfortable house in the whole of England, though it did have fabulous views over the Sludgelode valley and what was alleged to be a fragment of St Peter's loincloth in the family chapel. With any luck he would get another glimpse of the Countess.

He rolled over on the bed to see if there was a phone book. There was. There was no entry under 'Scarpington, Earl of', but several under 'Scarpington Estates'. What was the time? Crikey, approaching two. They'd probably be listening to the Archers. Best leave it till just after two and catch them before they go out and do whatever the nobility do on drizzling afternoons in the country. He lay back, thought briefly of England, and had another go at deciphering his notes.

All his instincts told him that the Artisans were rotten to the core. Yet that was grossly unfair. It was pure Londoner's prejudice, an Oxford-educated snobbery about trade, and a personal hang-up about golf and bridge. The Artisans were simply the provincial equivalent of one of the great City livery companies. He had no axe to grind about the Merchant Tailors or the Fishmongers or the Cordwainers; though come to think about it he did once have to investigate a particularly grubby murder which had occurred in the immediate aftermath of a great feast of the Worshipful Company of Harbingers. No, he was being silly, egged on by the lifelong chippiness of Detective Chief Inspector Wartnaby. Wartnaby was manifestly suffering from persecution mania. Nice chap in an eccentric way and obviously well read, widely travelled, particularly for an out of the way, end of the road dump like Scarpington but obviously not rational when it came to the local Establishment to which he so obviously did not belong. Come to think of it, Freddie seemed well travelled as well. Strange that in such an obviously one-eyed place, out of which you would not expect the average inhabitant to have moved at all, he should encounter two people who had knocked around as much as Wartnaby and the barman. It only went to show. God, what had he put in those cocktails? Brandy, gin, cointreau *and* Old Parsnip. No wonder he was feeling light-headed. Mind you, he hadn't eaten since breakfast and it was now almost two o'clock. That would explain it. Not that he was entirely sober. He was the first to admit it, always was. He wasn't the sort of 'social drinker' who couldn't face up to his addiction. Not a bit of it. Besides, it would have hindered his enquiries if he hadn't joined in. A certain amount of drinking was an essential concomitant of the job. You had to win people's confidence.

It was stuffy in the room and he went to open the window, only to find that it was one of the double-glazed unopening variety. An innovation of the new owner's, no doubt; a hallmark of Jolly Trenchermanship; a bit of Puce newbroomery. Out goes fusty old fresh air and in comes trendy new controlled environment.

There was a knock at the door. 'Room Service' called a male voice.

That was quick, he thought, and lurched over to let the waiter in.

He was a tall, athletic, vaguely eastern European youth in a cleaner version of Freddie's maroon jacket and black bow tie plus a plastic card over one nipple which said 'Frantisek'.

'Hi!' he said. 'I'm your Jolly Trencherman. One pint of Old Parsnip and a steak tartare with baked potato and sour cream.'

'But I asked for steak and chips.' Bognor did not wish to appear spoiled, petulant or drunk, but nevertheless he had definitely heard himself place the order.

'We regret that because of a problem in the kitchen it is not possible to prepare your steak as you had wished.'

'Well, what about the baked potato?' sighed Bognor. 'I asked for chips.'

'Microwave,' said Frantisek.

Oh well, he thought. At least that's honest. He signed the chit and sat down to eat.

He had forgotten how so much hunger could be brought on by a couple of drinks.

The steak tartare was little more than raw mince and egg, and the baked potato just cardboard sog. But the Old Parsnip went down well. He would have liked a cheroot when he finished, but he was supposed to have given up and Monica had booked them in to one of these new-fangled non-smoking bedrooms. He was not too sure about them. Unpleasant though he found other people's used smoke when it permeated the carpet and blankets, he did enjoy his own. But Monica had said 'no'. It was difficult having a bossy wife but there you were, it was a fact of his life.

He dialled the Scarpington Estates number which said 'Castle' by the side of it. It rang for an eternity and he was on the point of replacing the receiver in the manner of his first two attempts at room service when it was picked up and a voice said, 'Scarpington three thousand'. The voice was female and drawled.

'Could I speak to the Earl of Scarpington?'

'No.' The negative was drawn out into about three syllables and that was it. Nothing before, nothing after, just 'noooooo', exhaled down the line like dry ice. Bognor found himself tingling. He was a sucker for feminine hauteur.

'That *is* Scarpington Castle?'

'It is.'

'Could I, by any chance, be speaking to Lady Scarpington?'

'Yes,' she said, drawing the affirmative into even more syllables than the negative, and adding, 'You most certainly could.'

This was getting silly.

'When,' he asked, 'are you expecting Lord Scarpington?'

The voice suddenly became brisk. 'He's shooting with chums, so he won't be back till later. Can I help? To whom am I talking?'

'Um, Simon Bognor of the Board of Trade.'

'Goodness!'

Even through his own alcoholic haze Bognor was beginning to realise that the Countess, if indeed it was she, was not entirely herself either. If this was the case, he told himself, perhaps this was the time to strike. A squiffy wife might be prevailed upon to part with more family secrets than a sober one. Stood to reason.

'The fact of the matter,' he said, 'is that I'm trying to put together a sort of report thingy about Scarpington for

53

my boss and I'm at a bit of a loss as to how to set about it.
I really need someone to talk to.'

'Don't we all, darling!' exclaimed the Countess with
what sounded like considerable feeling.

'Perhaps if I were to come over you could fill me in
on one or two bits of information about Scarpington and
then your husband can fill me in on some others when he
gets back from his shooting.'

'Brill!' The Countess sounded pleased. 'Come to tea.
Mrs Perkins will have baked a cake, I dare say. Do you
play backgammon? Or bridge?'

'Neither, I'm afraid,' said Bognor.

'Thank God for that,' she said. 'I can see we're going to
have lots in common. I shall see you shortly, Mr er . . .'

'Bognor,' said Bognor.

'Of course. Come right on over, just as soon as you like.'

'I'll get a cab.'

'Just do that little thing.' And she gave a peal of laughter
and hung up.

'Dear God!' said Bognor out loud. He went next door
to the bathroom and splashed cold water all over his face,
while trying hard not to catch more than a glimpse of himself
in the mirror. He knew he wouldn't care for what he saw.
All mottled jowl. 'Oh ye wattles and dewlaps,' he said to
himself, 'praise him and magnify him for ever. I look like
a bloody turkey. The Countess will throw me out as soon
as look at me.'

Then he went back into the bedroom and wrote, in
a rather unsteady hand, under his wife's message: 'Gone
Castle see Mr and Mrs Scarps. Hope film good and you
unbored. Back soon. Luv S.'

There was always a line of taxicabs outside the Talbot
because it was the nearest approximation to a 'business'
and 'conference' hotel in town. This meant that it had
a fax machine and rooms with baize-covered boardroom
tables and what were now called 'audio-visual aids' but
which Bognor still thought of as 'magic lanterns' and associated with an agreeable old cove who used to come once

a year to his preparatory school in order to lecture on hedgehogs. It would be unreasonable to describe trade as brisk, but apart from Scarpington Lower Level which was the main-line Inter-City station and not to be confused with Scarpington Upper Level where the branch line to Stoke-on-Trent terminated, there was nowhere else for a taxi-driver to sensibly park.

His taxi-driver was not communicative. A thick-set, middle-aged man in a pseudo-leather jacket, he appeared to speak only in grunts. The back of his neck spilled over his collar and was pitted with scars which looked like the relics of a very serious and unpleasant childhood disease. Unless it was shrapnel. But he was too young for the last war and there seemed no good reason to suppose he had been involved in any sort of bombing. He was neither Irish nor Arabic and spoke – or rather grunted – in the unmistakable flat Scarpington accent. Bognor was unaware that there had ever been any incident in the town which could possibly account for shrapnel in the neck.

The drive out of town was as educational as anything he had yet accomplished on Parkinson's behalf. First the town centre – a mess of architectural styles ranging in antiquity from the 15th-century monastic conduit in front of the Victorian 'cathedral' which Monica had so disparaged to the rain-stained breezeblock of Marks and Spencer, Tesco, Next, Benetton, Laura Ashley and all the other chains which had so unified, homogenised, anaesthetised and generally screwed up the High Streets of England. In this matter Bognor was something of a fogey, an admirer, though with qualifications, of Prince Charles, Gavin Stamp and the late Sir John Betjeman.

In between these two extremes there were a few undistinguished Victorian relics, including the old Post Office, lovingly buffed up and scrubbed and floodlit. The Post Office was now a wine bar called 'Thingummys'. Some of the other refurbishments were inhabited by the twee-er, more Ashleyite chains. The Scarpington Society (patron Sir Seymour Puce) had been responsible for some new street signs with a William Morris lettering out of keeping with everything in sight and for some 'genuine antique' fibre-glass Edwardian lamp standards widely believed (though this had not been proved) to be manufactured by a dubious Puce subsidiary in Hong Kong.

Beyond the centre the themery swiftly disintegrated into ever crummier terraces of back-to-backs punctuated by Asian-run corner stores and video shops with latticed grilles over the windows. This was poor-white country, a land of fear and carpet slippers, the twitch of net curtain, the threat of hypothermia in the night, the exploding water heater, the toxic foam sofa, and all this punctuated by a government descant admonishing the natives to eat more greens and wear long johns.

It seemed much more than a mile from room service, however flawed, at the Talbot Hotel. Bognor thought of Frantisek and the steak tartare, gazed out at dull red brick, mortared by grime, and felt guilt. It was the guilt of the liberal privileged, an out of kilter, passé, sixties sentiment virtually unthinkable in the thrusting, hard-nosed self-support of Thatcher's Britain. But he felt it all the same.

Then suddenly it was Bangladesh. The same mean terraces became Dacca-sub-Sludgelode. Everywhere man was bearded and berobed and woman was swathed in sex-diminishing shapeless swaddle. Bognor was all in favour of the brotherhood of man, hail-fellow-well-met, same-again-thank-you-squire, don't-mind-if-I-do, say-what-you-like, and never a care if the drinker or speaker was a Hindu or a Jew or a Pole or a Turk speaking Urdu, Pushtu, Hindi, Hebrew, Burgess, Steiner or even plain old Middle English. Yet he was disconcerted by this clash of culture and architecture, this fervid contrast of faith and background and preconception. As they neared a railway bridge he glanced up and saw through the murk that someone had sprayed a slogan alongside the advertisement for Ferodo brake linings.

'Death to Rushdie!'

He shivered.

And then, seconds later, they were out of the city and on

a short strip of dual carriageway. Ahead, silhouetted against a pale peep of wintry afternoon sun, was the gaunt granite of one of the oldest inhabited homes in England, the domicile of d'eath-Stranglefields since the Conqueror had granted the land in 1068. Scarpington Castle.

Bognor sighed.

Behind that Gothic – Tennysonian Gothick, mind you – drawbridge and beneath that satellite dish gleaming pristine in the thin light of a December day was the Countess of Scarpington, pining while her husband the Earl was at the hunt. Well, shooting duck with the bank manager and Moulton the brewer or Sinclair the invalid carriage manufacturer. But who cared? The Earls of Scarpington had taken pleasure in the chase since time immemorial, while their ladies had taken their pleasures as they found them. Or something like that. Bognor, like the rest of the country, was becoming Disneyfied in old age. Other countries revised their history to suit present politics; the British were re-writing theirs as a series of pop-up books.

The castle was built on a curious excrescence not unlike a diminutive version of Glastonbury Tor. It was known officially as, 'Old Knob', and unofficially as 'The Stranglefield Wart'. It was an obvious place to build a Norman castle because the Knob or Wart was the only protuberance in the otherwise pan-flat Vale of Sludgelode. The original castle had been little more than a bleak, simple, four-square tower pocked with slits for firing arrows at anyone foolish enough to come galloping across the plain with hostile intent. Over the centuries it had been often besieged but never successfully. The worst moment had been during the Civil War. Scarpington itself had been for the parliamentarians, but Sir Blake d'eath-Stranglefield was a staunch monarchist. He and a small band of family and retainers held out against everything, including a severe biffing from cannon under the personal command of Cromwell himself.

In the domestically more docile eighteenth century, the family, elevated to the peerage by George III, attempted to soften the hawkish angularities of their ancestral abode.

Classical windows and wings and stable blocks were tacked on wherever possible and some estate workers' cottages at the foot of the Knob were demolished to make way for a water garden, a rose garden, an arboretum, a private zoo, a maze, and a deer park landscaped by a man said by some to be the ancestor of Stanley Green, the Artisan builder's merchant and known, inevitably, as Incapability Green. Actually Green had done a perfectly decent job, but no one could change the essential character of the Castle itself. The proper thing to have done – others, like the Digbys at Sherborne or the Cavendishes at Haddon managed it – would have been to abandon the old barrack fortress and build an entirely new mansion in a less commanding but more comfortable location. This was not the d'eath-Stranglefield way, which was why their modern successors were condemned to such damp and draughty grandeur.

The Castle was notionally open to the public, but at this time of year they had almost given up the pretence. The gates were closed and the taxi-driver had to conduct a grunted altercation with the lodge-keeper before gaining access. Bognor noticed a sign claiming that the zoo now boasted the world's largest collection of gerbils. Yet another sign of the decline in some aristocratic fortunes.

The drive up to the top of the Knob was narrow and steep; a north wind gusted in a flurry of sleet; high above the tallest turret the ancient banner of the Earls of Scarpington fluttered defiantly. 'Gormenghast,' muttered Bognor, as he grudgingly paid over twelve pounds to his driver who just as grudgingly gave him a receipt. Then he ran across the gravel to the *porte-cochère* where he yanked at a bellrope and waited, shivering.

Eventually a thin, elderly man in butler's gear opened the door and let him in, though without enthusiasm.

'Her ladyship is in the library,' he said. 'If you'll come this way.'

Bognor felt that he had been here before. Of course. McCrum Castle, home of Sir Archibald McCrum of that Ilk. He had had to go there when his investigations of the stately home industry, as it was then called – now they had become 'Historic Houses' – had turned nasty. Scarpington Castle had the same sense of being hewn from living granite, of outsize antlers above smoke-billowing fireplaces, of half-baked commercialism, of a desperate attempt to keep up appearances. Appearances of what, though, wondered Bognor, as he and the butler tip-tapped along echoing stone-flagged passages, past rusty armour, and family portraits so walnut with lacquer you could hardly make out the characteristic d'eath-Stranglefield noses in them. At last the butler paused before a closed oak door and knocked. Rather a bossy knock for a butler, thought Bognor.

From within a voice which managed to be simultaneously tinkling and husky said 'Come!' Just as on the phone, the single syllable was elongated into a protracted drawl. It was the drawing-room equivalent of the parade-ground trick of turning simple commands into a foghorn blast full seconds long.

'The gentleman from the Board of Trade,' said the butler to the back of a high, draught-excluding chair in front of the fire. From the size of the logs the fire was clearly meant to roar, but it only spat and fumed.

'Thank you, Perkins. That will be all. We don't want to be disturbed.'

'No, my lady.' Perkins withdrew gracelessly, giving Bognor a farewell glance which definitely said, 'Watch your step, sunshine.'

The voice from the chair now became flesh. The Countess of Scarpington was wearing skin-tight blue jeans, a black polo-neck sweater and brown cowboy boots. Her blonde hair which last night had been piled high under what must have been one of the few remaining family heirlooms now hung loose over her shoulders. As she stood to welcome her guest, she steadied herself against the chairback. Even as Bognor told himself that she really was incredibly sexy he also noticed that she was (a) not sober and (b) not as young as she had looked at dinner. Terrific paintwork and a remarkable figure could not, close to, disguise the fact that she was unlikely to see forty again. But then, thought Bognor, be reasonable. Nor will I.

'I say,' she said, 'isn't that an Arkwright and Blennerhasset?'

For a second he was confused, then he glanced down at his vivid tie. 'Yes, actually.'

'I say,' she said, clapping her hands in a gesture which was just a little too girlish. 'Did you know Bomber?'

'What?' said Bognor, raking through the embers of college life a quarter of a century before. 'You mean Jimmy Sprockett?'

'Absolutely.'

'God!' Bognor staggered slightly, and the Countess, by the merest flicker of attention, made him realise that she had noticed. 'Bomber Sprockett. Whatever happened to him?'

'Well,' she said, 'first he married me. Then he took me off to Australia where we not only had a ball but made a fortune in computers. And finally he went and got himself killed in the sea.'

'Oh dear,' said Bognor. He couldn't think of anything better.

'They never found him. He was out on the reef snorkelling. It could have been a shark, I suppose. Silly old Sprockett. So anyway I came home with the loot and married an earl.'

'Oh.'

'I think this calls for a celebration,' she said. 'In fact I was thinking it would probably call for a celebration anyway so rather than have boring tea and boring cake made by boring Mrs Perkins I thought we'd have some of Piggy's seriously interesting champagne. Luckily for us he just happens to keep two or three bottles in the fridge up here for just such emergencies so we don't have to disturb Perkins and get him to go and rummage in the cellar.'

She sashayed over to the panelling under a picture of the fourth Earl, 'Black Jack Stranglefield', and did something nifty which caused a door to swing open and reveal a small fridge full of bottles. Out came a bottle of Veuve Clicquot '82.

'Piggy's something called "A Friend of the Widow" which

means he gets a bottle of bubbly every birthday.' She wrinkled her nose. 'Non-vintage, though, which I think is rather vulgar.' She pointed to a cabinet in the corner. 'Glasses over there. Will you do it or shall I?'

Bognor did it, managing to screw the cork off with the merest of dull pops and not spilling a drop.

'Take a pew,' she said, settling back into her chair.

Bognor sagged into an enormous sofa opposite.

'Cheers,' she said. 'Isn't this fun?'

'Cheers,' said Bognor. 'Tremendous fun.'

'And fancy you knowing Sprockett!'

'Yes, fancy.'

She smiled at him. Her own teeth, gap in the middle. Crow's feet at the corners of the eye.

'But you don't know Piggy?'

'No, not yet.'

She drank a little champagne and looked up at him from under a mane of blonde. 'I hope you don't mind my asking,' she said, removing a wayward hair which momentarily blurred her vision, 'but have you been drinking?'

'Yes, actually.'

She giggled. 'Well, that's rather a relief. So have I. So that makes two of us.'

She stared at him.

Bognor stared back.

After a longer than comfortable mutual stare, she said, as if consciously flipping back into conventional gear, 'You said you were writing some sort of report about Scarpington.'

'Yes.' Bognor sketched in the essential details and she listened, wide-eyed.

'What an assignment!' she said, when he'd finished. 'Poor you. This place is the absolute pits.'

'Oh,' said Bognor. 'It surely isn't as bad as all that.'

'I can assure you,' she said, 'it is every bit as bad as all that. Thank Christ I kept on the flat in Eaton Square.'

'My boss seems to think Scarpington is rather like everywhere else except London,' said Bognor. 'That's why he chose it.'

'If he really thought that then he could have chosen anywhere else instead, couldn't he?' She tossed her head to get rid of more hair in the eyes. 'And I can assure you anywhere else would have been an infinitely more amusing place.'

'Unfortunately my boss doesn't pay for me to be amused.' Bognor spoke with all the resentment of a man whose career has passed lunch and settled into early afternoon.

'Funny thing,' she said, glancing towards the window which was taking a terrible lashing from the storm. 'Most people here seem to think Piggy married me for my looks.'

'And he didn't?' This was meant as a compliment, albeit heavy-handed. She acknowledged it with another sideways grin. 'No,' she said. 'Piggy married me for the lolly and I married him for the title. Bloody silly thing to do but I think I'll hang in. Would you hang in if it were you? I mean, I'm hardly ever here, and he's hardly ever in town.'

'Is there enough money?'

She laughed. 'There's enough money,' she said, 'even with this great millstone to subsidise. In fact once I'd got my accountants on to the estate it's surprising how little money it need actually lose. And we think we've struck oil on one of the farms. Literally, I mean. So in the end I may even make money out of the deal. Which would be ironic, don't you think?'

'I suppose so.'

'You were at the dinner last night,' she said suddenly.

'Yes.'

'With a woman who looked like a horse.'

'My wife.'

'Sorry. I didn't mean to be rude. She looked like a very nice horse. Some people are very attracted to horses. Wasn't it Joyce Grenfell who said that the world was divided into horses and buttons?'

'Sounds like her,' said Bognor, and then, wishing to change the subject because talk of Monica was making him feel guilty even though, of course, he was only here out of duty, he said, 'Quite dramatic, that chap Brackett keeling over like that. I'd only just met him. He was one of the first Scarpingtonians I'd been to see.'

'Grubby little man,' she said. 'Oddly enough, he'd been to visit Piggy only yesterday morning.'

'Really.' Even through the fuzz of booze Bognor's antennae twitched. 'Were they mates?'

'God knows,' said the Countess, 'but they were fellow Artisans, and in Scarpington terms that means more than family, more than the Old Boy Network, more than, oh, I don't know . . .' She poured more champagne. The champagne was disappearing fast but there was more in the fridge. Whether it was that or the thought of the Artisans was difficult to tell but her voice had suddenly taken on a note of hysteria and for a moment Bognor was appalled to realise that she was on the verge of tears.

'I was beginning to form that impression already,' he said. 'I had a session this morning with Freddie, the barman at the St Moritz bar . . .'

'Him!' Lady Scarpington's control again teetered on the brink. 'Now there really is something quite unbelievably creepy about him. The way he looks at women. Ugh! And he know too much. He reeks of other people's sad, sad secrets.'

'You were saying about Brackett . . .'

'Was I?'

'About his visit. Coming to see your husband.'

She visibly made an effort to take a grip. 'Do you mind if I take my boots off,' she asked. 'In fact, would you awfully mind pulling them off for me? They're rather tight.' And she lifted one of her skinny, shapely legs in his direction. Bognor swallowed hard, got to his feet, and performed this delicate task while trying to pretend that he derived no physical satisfaction from it whatsoever. Afterwards he went back to his sofa while she curled up and tucked her feet under her bottom. He couldn't help noticing that she had painted toenails and a gold chain round her left ankle. Monica was always intensely disparaging about women who wore chains round their ankles. But he must, he told himself severely, banish all thought of Monica and concentrate on his professional investigations.

'You say,' he said, trying to sound brisk and under control, 'you say that your husband and Reg Brackett had a meeting.'

'Not a very amicable meeting,' she said. 'In fact, something very close to a row. I've seldom seen Piggy so agitated. Not like him. He's normally so wet you could shoot snipe off him.'

'What was the row about?'

'God knows.' She said it as if she not only did not know but was past caring.

'Your husband didn't have anything to do with Bracketts Laundry and Dry Cleaning Services?'

'Good grief, no! He wasn't even a customer. We do all that sort of stuff in-house.' She rearranged her feet. 'I do know he wanted money.'

'How do you know that?'

'Because Piggy asked me for money.'

Bognor thought for a moment and poured them both another glass. Almost without noticing they had killed the bottle.

'If you don't mind me asking, what are your, er, financial arrangements?'

'We don't have a joint account,' she said. 'I wouldn't share an account with my dear husband any more than I'd share a bed, frankly. I give him a regular allowance. Anything over and above that he has to ask. Sometimes I give, sometimes I don't.'

'So if he needs to acquire a new and exotic gerbil the Earl would have to borrow from you?'

She grinned. 'I've told him the gerbils must go. Some smart alec has latched on to the idea that there are one or two peers of the realm who are a bit lacking in the brain department, so he's cleaned up selling bogus tourist attractions to half the stately home owners in Britain. Piggy got the gerbils. It could have been worse. The McCrum of that Ilk has got sporrans.'

'Wouldn't you know it?' Bognor grinned back. 'The world's biggest collection of sporrans. I used to know the McCrum. He's mad.'

'So's Piggy. In a negative sort of way. Anyway, Brackett was after my money and I said "no". I don't think Piggy had expected anything else. The only thing I would say is that I think Brackett was doing more than just ask.'

'Beg, you mean? A bended knee job?'

'No, more than that.' She frowned. 'I think he threatened. I think it was money with menaces. He must have been desperate, if so. One Artisan threatening another. Unthinkable.' She arched her eyebrows.

'Breaking the Artisan oath.'

'Absolutely.' She ran a finger along the gold chain at her ankle and flexed her painted toes, then looked at her watch which was a chunky and very expensive one-off Cartier. Poor dead Sprockett's computer business must, thought Bognor, have been extraordinarily successful. Funny, he had always thought of Sprockett as rather dim. Certainly dimmer than himself. It only went to show.

The Countess leaned back and half yawned, half purred.

'Piggy won't be back for an age,' she said. 'Do you think we ought to have the other half?' She nodded towards the empty Widow's cruse.

'I don't know that I could.' Bognor knew that he had had more than enough, but he was always easily tempted, particularly when, as now, his defences were down.

'I'll tell you what,' she said. 'One of the little luxuries I have allowed is a sauna and the tiniest little indoor pool you've ever seen in your life. What would you say to that? It would help us sober up.'

'Not,' said Bognor, with a perceptiveness which surprised him, 'if we have the other half.'

'Well,' she said, 'at least they'll cancel each other out.'

'Do you reckon?'

'Well,' her smile was almost absurdly arch this time, 'it's a theory. We won't know until we put it to the test will we?'

'I don't have any swimming trunks.'

Her smile this time quite plainly said that to talk of swimming trunks in a developing situation such as this was mere prudery. But sensing, correctly, that prudery, though mixed with prurience, was an essential part of Bognor's nature, she said, 'I'm sure I can find you a pair of Piggy's.'

'Are you sure it's safe?' Bognor knew perfectly well it wasn't in the least safe, but it was amazing what excess alcohol could do for a chap, even one as safety-conscious as he was.

'Safe?' This time there was no mistaking the sexual inflection. She was thinking about AIDS and herpes and condoms and other hitherto unmentionables which now, to Bognor's consternation, seemed to have become a regular part of chit-chat in even the most polite society.

'Heart,' said Bognor, deliberately misunderstanding. 'I mean, I haven't checked but I have a nasty feeling my blood pressure isn't what it should be. And I am a pound or two overweight.' (For 'pound', he thought, read 'stone'.) 'And don't they say it's particularly dangerous if you've been drinking?'

'Do they?' She purred again. 'I always think it's even more fun after drinking. And if the worst came to the worst, what a way to go! Better than being eaten by sharks like poor Sprockett. And I'm rather fabulous at mouth-to-mouth resuscitation. Or so I'm told.'

Oh God, oh Monica, thought Bognor to himself, what's going on? I'm out of control. I'm not in charge. Help and yet not help!

As if in answer to this silent, if confused supplication, the phone sitting on an ancient chest which looked as if it might have accompanied Sir Ralph d'eath-Stranglefield on the Crusades began to ring. The Countess looked at it, ⁓⁓ ⁓⁓ed at him. Bognor looked at it, and then at the

⁓ should just let it ring.'

⁓ t he was lost.

It rang for quite some time and they both could almost feel its exasperation before eventually with a petulant final yelp it cut off.

'I'll find you some trunks,' she said. 'Won't be a jiffy. Just wait here and don't go away.'

Bognor wondered where on earth she expected him to go.

She was away for about five minutes and such was Bognor's state that it seemed on the one hand much longer and on the other shorter. Perhaps, he thought, that was what was meant by the left and right side of the brain. A different perception of time. The rain drummed against the leaded window pane. He thought of Reg Brackett and his last unfinished joke. He thought of Scarpington Specials and the barman's friend. He thought of Monica and tried not to. He thought of the Countess's painted toenails. He wondered what Parkinson would say. And smiled.

'Here,' she said, shimmying up behind him unheard in bare feet and a white towelling robe. 'Try these for size.'

Piggy Scarpington, whom Bognor had only ever seen sitting down, evidently had a lot of bottom. The trunks, scarlet with a gold S and coronet on the right buttock, looked as if they would have fitted the hind legs of a pantomime rhinoceros.

Diana Scarpington marginally misinterpreted Bognor's embarrassment. 'I won't look,' she said, and strode to the windows where she lit a cigarette and stared with exaggerated disinterest at the weather.

'What a bloody awful day,' she said, blowing smoke at the glass. 'Until you turned up, that is. Fancy your knowing poor Sprockett.'

'You can turn round now,' said Bognor. He felt more than usually silly in Lord Scarpington's scarlet trunks, particularly as he was still wearing his tweed jacket and the purple and pink A and B tie.

'Oh, you look absolutely adorable,' said his hostess, turning and laughing. 'I'll bring the glasses if you bring the bottle. Follow me.' And she led the way, still laughing in be humming what sounded, sort of, like the famous tenor aria from *Don Giovanni*.

More flagstoned corridor. There seemed no end to them. Bognor, carrying his shoes, trousers and an unopened bottle of vintage champagne, was glad there was no one there to see him. Was it merely imagination which made him think that whole generations of d'eath–Stranglefield ancestors were looking down the collective family nose as they passed? On balance he thought not.

'It's a long way down,' she said, stopping at the end of one of the interminable, dripping corridors, 'so we installed a lift.' She pressed a button and the wall slid to one side. It was a very small lift with the result that they were cabin'd, cribb'd, and confined to such an extent that they were compelled to touch. Bognor's hands were full. The Countess had two glasses in one and with the other first pressed the 'Down' button, and then found the back of Bognor's neck and pulled his mouth down on to hers. It was obvious to Bognor, drunk though he was, that she had done this sort of thing before.

'Mmmmm,' she said, as the lift touched bottom with a bump. 'You taste as if you've been drinking.'

Bognor was feeling rather sick. He hoped he was going to be all right. It had been a bumpy ride. Somewhere nearby a phone began to ring. Diana Scarpington picked up a receiver on the wall just outside the lift, said snappily, 'Wrong number' and replaced it.

'Here we are, then,' she said, unnecessarily. 'What do you think?'

It was certainly a contrast with the rest of the leaky old Schloss, though he was surprised to see that one or two relics of the dungeon's former use remained. There were manacles attached to a wall; a sort of stocks; and something that looked like a thumbscrew.

'Piggy has such a sense of history,' said the Countess, 'so They're inclined to give me the creeps, but what 's inebriated gaze they had a suspiciously st as if they had been put to use quite

The rest of the dungeon was quite different. There was a pine-finished area to the right which already gave off the throat-burning aroma of sauna heat; to the left a placid round pool which looked icy cool; and between the two a foaming sauna. Sprinkled about the place were leather-covered cushions, sofas and bean bags. On one wall there was a screen. Opposite, a hole in the wall.

'Projector?' he enquired. 'Absolutely,' she said. 'You can sit in the jacuzzi and watch whatever you want. Bliss.'

She removed the robe in slow, seductive movements. Underneath she was wearing the skimpiest conceivable bikini, little more than a purple G-string with two tiny purple half-moons barely concealing her nipples.

'Don't you think,' she said, 'you ought to take off your jacket and tie? It's terribly hot in there.'

Again she moved in close. This time she slipped off his tweed coat with an almost professional dexterity, then unknotted his tie, unbuttoned his shirt buttons and slid both hands under the shirt.

'I bet you don't get this at home,' she said, pressing her mouth to his. 'Mmmm!'

An eternity later she released him. 'I don't think you're in training,' she said, with just a hint of peevishness. 'Come on, bring the bottle.' And she grabbed him by the hand and led him into the broilerhouse. Once inside she closed the door and scooped water on to a bucket of what Bognor took to be white-hot coals. As the steam caught him full in the mouth he found himself gagging and gasping for breath.

'Christ!' he said eventually.

She laughed and opened the champagne as easily as she had removed his jacket and tie. 'Have a drink,' she said, and poured. 'Lie down, take it easy.' She herself eased on to one of the wooden slatted bunks and wriggled off her miniscule bikini-top. 'Mmmm,' she said. 'Isn't this just heaven?'

Bognor was still finding breath hard to come by. He didn't know how much of this heat torture he could stand. Cardiac arrest under these circumstances would be embarrassing. Perhaps he should have stayed upstairs. He lay back and tried breathing very slowly and regularly. It seemed to work because the next thing he knew the Countess was shaking him, with a look half-way between irritation and anxiety.

'Come on,' she said, evidently relieved to find him still alive. 'You need a plunge.' So saying, she yanked him upright with surprising force and pulled him out of the sauna across the floor and into the cold pool.

It was very deep and they seemed to go down for ever. Bognor decided that he was dead. He had never, well hardly ever, experienced such a shock to the system. He had no wind left in his body at all. From the oven into the refrigerator. He felt like a Christmas turkey shoved still frozen into the Aga. No, that was the wrong way round. Like a Baked Alaska thrust under the grill.

And then they were going up and up and then they broke through the surface and they were back in the torture chamber dungeon and he wasn't dead after all, just suffering terribly and beyond breath, and quite unable to appreciate the sleek, almost naked albeit middle-aged charms of the fiendish woman who was doing all these things to him. He was going to freeze.

'Help!' he whispered. 'Help!' Whereupon she pulled him up and out and propelled him into the jacuzzi. Oh, that was better! He found himself almost smiling. She had positioned him on a submerged seat so that only his head and shoulders stuck out of the comfortable warm water. A throbbing jet of water massaged the small of his back from behind. Diana Scarpington had vanished, but a second later she was back with the bottle and the two glasses and she too subsided languorously into the jacuzzi.

'Golly,' said Bognor, 'that was a *mauvais quart d'heure*.'

'Don't be so feeble,' she said. 'You sound as wet as Piggy.'

She poured two glasses. 'Chin-chin,' she said, and, sitting gently on his lap, put both arms round him, pulled their bodies close together and started to kiss him with an animal urgency he was almost certain he had never before experienced.

'Sssh!' he said, just as he feared he would choke on her tongue or bleed to death from the sharp clamp of her teeth on his lips. 'Shhh! I can hear something. It's the lift. Listen. Someone's using the lift.'

But she was beyond listening. He could feel her heart pounding against his; her fingernails grinding into his shoulder blades and kidneys; her tongue . . . and then, just as he thought everything had to be a dream, he saw the door from the lift shaft open, and people enter the dungeon. The people were familiar. Some more so than others. He only just recognised the butler and would probably not have done so but for his pinstripe trousers and black jacket and the expression which said 'Gotcha, sunshine!' He recognised the Earl of Scarpington from the night before and he recognised Detective Inspector Wartnaby from breakfast.

As for Monica . . .

'Oh God!' he said.

CHAPTER FIVE

Not a Tremendously Good Show

Monica Bognor dropped another brace of Alka-Seltzer into a plastic mug and regarded her husband with a gaze that would have sunk the *Bismarck*.

'It's no use, Simon,' she said. '*In flagrante* is *in flagrante*. I saw you. Her husband saw you. Detective Chief Inspector Wartnaby saw you. And, worst of all, the butler saw you.'

Bognor, sitting on the bed, moaned softly.

'And you will get absolutely no sympathy by making ridiculous noises. You merely diminish yourself still further. If such a thing were possible. Now drink this.'

Bognor stretched out a hand and took the plastic mug. He knew it would only make him sick again but he deserved it. He would never touch alcohol again. Never. Nor let another woman past his lips.

'I am fed up,' continued Mrs Bognor. 'I am fed up with you. I am fed up with Scarpington. I am fed up with life. I am catching the ten o'clock train and I am going home. When I am home I shall think. If you don't hear from me, you'll be hearing from my solicitors.'

Bognor drank the Alka-Seltzer.

'I—' he began, but was unable to get any further, partly because he felt too ill and partly because his wife interrupted him too quickly.

'Don't even think about speaking. The woman is notorious. You must have known that before you went there. And her poor unfortunate husband. I thought I knew you,

72

Simon Bognor, but I was wrong. I knew you were weak; I knew you were easily led; I knew you were stupid; but I did not realise that you were vicious and venal.'

It was no use. Bognor had to be sick. He rushed to the bathroom and crumpled in a kneeling position in front of the lavatory bowl. He had not felt so awful for years. It must have been the room service steak tartare. Unfortunately he had vomited up that in a ditch half-way between the castle and the hotel. Thank heaven they had stopped Wartnaby's car in time. It would have been even worse if he had been sick over that.

A few minutes later he felt able to return to the bedroom.

'Seriously, darling, I really do think Freddie could have stuck me with a Micky Finn. He had this thing, a cross between a nose dropper and a water pistol. It was given to him by a friend on the *Queen Mary*.'

'Don't you "darling" me, Simon. I am not in the mood for forgiveness.' She was tapping her finger on the table. Metronomically. It was a very bad sign indeed. 'And I think it is cheap, cheap even by your shoddy standards, to blame your disgrace on a dead man who is unable to speak for himself.'

There was some truth in this.

Freddie was dead. It was the reason for the unexpected arrival of Monica and Wartnaby. That afternoon, not more than an hour after Bognor had left him, the neighbours had reported a fire in Freddie's grotty little flat in the 'poor white' section of town through which Bognor had been driven in his taxi.

By the time the fire brigade had broken down the front door Freddie was dead. Very. Wartnaby had been notified of the death and seen enough at first glance to view it as suspicious and, given his earlier conversation with Bognor, probably relevant to his enquiries regarding Brackett. He had rung the Talbot and found Monica, just returned from an unsatisfactory afternoon watching a bad print of a movie which, as a result of some uncharacteristic failure of internal wiring, she had expected to be a Louis Malle but which was actually a Michael Winner.

She had told Bert Wartnaby that Bognor had left a note saying he was Castle-bound so Wartnaby had phoned twice. On getting no reply, or rather one 'no reply' and one 'wrong number', he had called Monica again. She, concerned, had asked to go with him. On arrival they had bumped into the Earl on the drawbridge. He, incidentally, smelt strongly of Miss Dior (identified by Monica) and did not look in the least like a man who had just come in from the shoot. Indeed he looked pretty shifty. The three, entering together, were confronted by the butler, Perkins, who was evidently all too eager to connive at the come-uppance of the Countess and a guest to whom he had clearly taken an instant aversion.

'I do believe m'lady said something about a medicinal sauna,' he had said, or some such pseudo-sycophantic hypocrisy. So they had all crammed into the intimacy of an elevator made for two and burst in on Bognor and the Countess practically naked, and intimately entwined in the hot tub. End of story. Or of chapter.

Secretly, of course, Monica was not altogether surprised nor even as cross as she had seemed. In a way she was relieved because it gave her an excuse for escaping from a provincial city which she was finding every bit as bloody as the Countess. And she knew that there was no malice in her wretch of a husband. It was just that a certain sort of woman, herself included should the truth be told, found him peculiarly cuddly. Of course he was exasperating. Of course he was pathetic. Of course he was easily led. But these were negative vices and against them Bognor had some positive virtues even if, for the moment, she could not recall what they were. Cuddliness was one. Vulnerability another. Oh well, what the hell, she was fond of him, and he, she knew, of her. Despite occasional appearances to the contrary. Besides, there was a certain bizarre satisfaction in having your husband snatched by someone quite as exotic as the Countess of Scarpington. Still Monica had observed, with unspoken pride, that while she was undeniably in good shape for a woman of her age, her breasts were distinctly scrawny. Monica considered hers definitely superior.

And she had to concede that her spouse, now sitting green upon the hotel bed, did look impossibly sad and ill. Not, however, attractive enough, or contrite enough, to be forgiven just yet. And she was damned if she was going to stay in this provincial hell-hole a moment longer. So she would be on the ten o'clock to King's Cross and let him stew. She would allow herself to be taken out for an expensive dinner by one of her handful of attentive, and rich, exes. And when she did finally deign to talk to Simon again she would let him know. She would even suggest that she too had dallied and strayed, perhaps to rather more effect than he had managed in the castle dungeon sauna.

'Very well,' she said, zipping her bag shut with a finality as withering as weed-killer. 'I'm off. I suggest you have an extremely good night's sleep and start off tomorrow with as clean a sheet as you can contrive. But don't expect me to forgive. Or to forget. It is my opinion that you are beneath contempt.' She looked at him properly for a second and to herself, silently, said, 'Oh, Simon, Simon, who is your own worst enemy? You are such a silly little boy.' And out loud: 'I wouldn't look in the mirror tomorrow morning. You might frighten yourself to death.'

She strode to the door, opened it, and turned with one final theatrical toss of the head.

'Don't ring me,' she threw back at him. 'I'll ring you.'

Bognor tried to respond, but the words, whatever they were, would not come.

She flounced out, crashing the door behind her.

'Silly sod,' she said.

So Bognor slept alone that night. He did not enjoy it, but he slept the sleep of the dead, or the damned – dreamless and undisturbed. When he woke, it was to a knocking at the door.

'Room Service,' came the call, reminding him all too vividly of the events of the day before.

He bundled himself out of bed, realising to his surprise and chagrin that he was still in his shirtsleeves and underpants, lurched to the door, opened it and found Osbert Wartnaby standing there with a tray and a clutch of newspapers.

'What happened to Frantisek?' asked Bognor, confused.

'Who?' Wartnaby seemed as confused. 'I thought you'd need a proper breakfast so I've brought you the works. Charming girl called Miriam in the kitchen. I've charged it to your bill.'

'Oh.' Bognor stroked stubble and wondered why he was not feeling more hung-over. Probably still drunk. The hangover would strike around eleven, just when he was least expecting it. That was the way with hangovers. They were like clever muggers, always attacking you when your guard was down.

'I must say I have to hand it to you.' Bognor contemplated the tray. A *cafetière* of what looked like proper coffee, eggs, bacon, black pudding, fried bread, orange juice, thick toast, butter, Baxter's. 'This looks like the real McCoy. How do you do it?'

Wartnaby smiled. 'It's amazing,' he said, 'the effect an official police identity card has on the average citizen. Very gratifying. Good to know that despite what one reads in the press there is an inherent respect for the law among Joe Public.'

'Absolutely.' Bognor took his dressing gown – silk, paisley, a gift from Monica – off the peg on the door and tied the belt round his waist. It gave him at least a semblance of dignity.

'I'm sorry about yesterday,' he said.

'No problem,' said Wartnaby. 'My fault, in a way. I should have warned you what a man-eater the Countess is.'

'I hope ... er ... I mean, your car. I seem to remember being unwell on the way home.' It had been an unmarked car, Wartnaby's own. If he had fouled it Wartnaby would presumably have had to clean it up himself.

'Perfectly all right,' he said, pouring out two cups from the *cafetière*. 'I took the liberty of bringing in my own coffee. Higgins's very own Kibo Chagga. Miriam didn't seem to object.'

Bognor took a sip. It was very good.

'How are you feeling?' Wartnaby seemed genuinely solicitous.

'Fine,' said Bognor. 'I seem to remember Monica dosing me very heavily with Alka-Seltzer before she left.'

'Left?'

'She caught the ten o'clock train back to town.'

'She would, wouldn't she,' said Wartnaby as Bognor tucked in ravenously. The black pudding was especially succulent. He adored black pudding. For a second it took his mind off marital problems.

'She'll be back, though,' said Wartnaby.

'You reckon?' Bognor's mouth was full. He swallowed. 'I wouldn't bank on it. Monica's got iron resolution.'

'I could see that, even on our short acquaintance. But speaking as something of an authority on the matter of the sexual tiff I can assure you she'll be back. Maybe not to Scarpington but certainly to you.'

'Good,' said Bognor, not really convinced even though he was impressed by Wartnaby's certainty and his man-of-the-worldliness. 'Do you think I should apologise to the Earl?'

'Absolutely not,' said Wartnaby. 'First of all, we got there in the nick of time so no actual intimacy took place. And secondly it happens all the time so there'll be someone else in a day or two. In any case, he didn't seem in the least put out. In fact, if it hadn't been for me and the butler and Mrs Bognor I dare say he'd have sat down and watched while you got on with it.'

'Good grief!' Bognor stopped in mid-mouthful. 'Do you really think so?'

'You learn to spot that sort of thing when you've been in the force as long as I have,' said Wartnaby. He smiled.

Bognor ate on in silence.

Presently he said, 'What about Freddie? You say he's dead. What exactly happened?'

'Ah.' The Detective Chief Inspector became grave. 'We have a problem there,' he said. 'A very serious problem.'

'Oh, dear.' Bognor also put on an expression designed to indicate extreme *gravitas*. It actually just had the effect of making him look stuffed, but it was the only serious expression he had.

'It's what I feared,' said Wartnaby. 'First thing this morning I was summoned by my Chief Constable and told I was off the case.'

'You're joking.'

'Afraid not.'

'But they can't do that.' Bognor was almost more outraged than the DCI.

'In Scarpington they can.'

'But for what reason?'

'A chief constable isn't required to give reasons,' said Wartnaby. 'Not even to senior detective officers on his pay roll. Officially he says that the pathologist's report shows that Brackett had a heart attack. Well, of course, you and I know better than that, don't we?'

'Absolutely,' said Bognor. 'Freddie fixed him with that little water pistol job.'

'Spot on,' said Wartnaby. 'With which I suspect he also spiked your cocktails, thus inducing such uncharacteristic behaviour.'

'It had crossed my mind.' Bognor pushed the empty plate to one side and buttered some toast. 'Do you think he was trying to kill me too?'

'I doubt it.' Wartnaby stroked his jaw. 'I suspect he was just trying to warn you off.'

'But what about Freddie? Who killed him?'

'I suspect we shall never know,' said Wartnaby.

'But why not? I mean it doesn't make sense. You're the investigating officer.'

'My Chief Constable doesn't think there's anything to investigate. He's had the scene of crime report and he takes the view, or rather he says he takes the view, that our friend Freddie set fire to himself while drunk.'

'And that's it?'

'That's it.' Wartnaby stood. His suit was sharper than

yesterday's. Almost presentable. 'Not only am I off the case, I'm suspended.'

Bognor was shocked. 'But that's deplorable. What are you going to do?'

Wartnaby sighed. 'There's very little I can do. Or could do if it wasn't for you, thank heaven.'

'I'll protest at once,' said Bognor. 'I'll have you reinstated in a jiffy. My boss Parkinson is not without influence. I'll get him to phone your Chief Constable and tell him what's what p.d.q.'

'No, no.' Wartnaby held both hands up in a restraining gesture. 'We have to keep very calm. The point is that, as I suspected, my Chief Constable is being hushed up by Puce and the Artisans.'

Bognor nodded. It made sense. In a corrupt community the Chief of Police was always bent. Well-known fact.

'Is he a member, your Chief Constable?'

'No. Not an actual member. But heavily under the influence. As I told you, Puce has this town completely sewn up.'

'I didn't realise it was as bad as that,' said Bognor.

'Every bit.' Wartnaby smiled grimly. 'But luckily we have you to fall back on.'

Bognor frowned. 'I'm not entirely with you,' he said.

'Oh, yes, you are, thank God. That's exactly what you are. Together we'll see this thing through, if it's the last thing we do. Do you want truth and justice to prevail or not?'

'Oh very much,' agreed Bognor, who despite a certain lassitude was, broadly speaking, on the side of truth and justice provided they did not get in the way of a quiet life. 'So what do we do?'

'What you do,' said Wartnaby, 'is to carry on as before. Nobody's taken you off the case. Or had you suspended. I'll brief you every morning at breakfast. Otherwise I'm going to lie extremely low. If my Chief Constable even begins to suspect that I'm maintaining any interest in the case he'll have my guts for garters, as they used to say in the Army.'

Bognor thought for a moment. It was all a bit irregular, but not seriously so. Wartnaby would help him complete his Board of Trade study by supplying inside gen, just as he had originally promised. If, in return, he could help an honest cop eradicate the cancer in the heart of local society, then that was a useful by-product.

'You're on,' he said, wiping his lips with a Jolly Trencherman paper napkin.

'Good man,' said Wartnaby.

'Now if I'm right,' said the DCI, 'and I'm seldom wrong, we're dealing here with a serial killer who has struck twice in twenty-four hours. What does that say to you?'

'One, that we're dealing with some sort of maniac,' said Bognor, 'and two, that he's likely to kill again.'

'I'd say you're right on both counts. Now . . .' Wartnaby took from his inside jacket pocket a single sheet of lined paper. The writing was shaky and semi-literate. It was headed '"Bridge". League B. November 17th.' Underneath were four names and alongside them were numbers. They read as follows:

      Brown D. 3
      Moulton A. 2
      Festing A. 7
      Fothergill H. 9

Bognor thought. 'Jolly peculiar,' he said, after a while. 'I mean, on the face of it, it looks as if this is the result of November 17th's bridge rubbers, but I thought you played bridge in pairs.'

'Quite so,' said Wartnaby.

'So why has everyone got a different score?'

'It's conceivable,' said Wartnaby, 'that they swapped partners half-way through.'

Bognor's cardsharping went about as far as Snap and Beggar My Neighbour. Nor was he at his forensic best this morning.

'I'd better write this down myself,' he said, and got

out his notebook. 'OK,' he said. 'First of all, who are these people? Moulton is presumably the brewer and Brown the dairy owner, Festing the solicitor and Fothergill is my friend Harold, the Rupert Murdoch of Scarpington.'

'Not quite,' said Wartnaby. 'You're right about Moulton and Fothergill, but not the other two. Festing's first name is Nigel and Brown's is Ron.'

'Funny,' said Bognor. 'It says Festings A. and Brown D.'

'Unfair of me.' Wartnaby looked smug. 'This is where local knowledge comes in handy. Nigel Festing's wife is Angela and Brown's is Dorothy.'

'Ah!' said Bognor. 'So we're talking about a bridge four comprising Mr Fothergill, Mr Moulton, Dorothy Brown and Angela Festing.'

'It looks very much like it.' Wartnaby went to the double-glazed window and looked across the city. 'With the working classes it's drink; with the upper classes it's sex; and with the middle it's bridge. Or so my grandmother always maintained.'

'The Jewish one?'

Wartnaby turned and smiled. 'You remembered. Yes. I wonder if she was right.'

'So,' said Bognor, looking at the paper. The problem was beginning to resemble one of those tricky questions that had scuppered his first attempt on elementary mathematics at 'O' level. 'If Augustus Moulton has two points, Dorothy Brown three and Angela Festing seven, how many points does Harold Fothergill have?' He frowned furiously. 'Let's assume,' said Bognor, 'that the blokes played the girls for the first rubber and won. That means they get one apiece and the girls nothing.' He carefully pencilled the figure one against Fothergill and Moulton and left the other two blank. 'Next round Moulton and Festing play Fothergill and Brown and the Moulton team win. So at the end of round two Moulton has two points, Fothergill and Festing one each and Brown nought.' He jotted down the numbers. 'I think I've cracked it,' he said with an air of triumph.

'That's what I thought at first,' said Wartnaby, 'but it doesn't work.'

'Why not?' Bognor was sweating. He had not shaved yet, he remembered, nor bathed or washed. He was definitely a bit smelly. Wartnaby smelled too, but his niff was something deliberate. Lavender, he thought, though he wasn't too hot on smells. Monica would be able to identify it immediately. His own niff, on the other hand, was animal and inadvertent. As soon as his visitor went he would have a luxurious soak in the bath with a liberal dose of the Jolly Trencherman bath oil so thoughtfully supplied in a one-shot sachet.

'Because,' said Wartnaby, 'the numbers don't add up to an even total. They come to twenty-one.'

'Hang on,' said Bognor. 'Two plus three is five. Plus seven is twelve. Plus nine is twenty-one. So what does that prove?'

'It proves the scoring wasn't done like that.'

Bognor scratched an armpit absent-mindedly. 'Are you sure?'

'Of course.' The Inspector sounded quite tetchy. 'Work it out for yourself. If two of them got a point for every win then it would have to be an even number total.'

'Oh, all right,' said Bognor, tetchy himself, 'so maybe it was three for a win and two for a draw.'

'You can't draw at bridge.'

'Are you sure?'

'Positive.' Wartnaby seemed enviably certain. Once more Bognor wished Monica was with him for confirmation. She had played bridge when she was young. She knew about such things.

'So they were playing some other game.' Bognor thought. 'Poker, perhaps.'

'Maybe,' said Wartnaby. 'Now why do you imagine the score sheet – if it *is* a score sheet – was in Freddie's flat?'

'That bothers me too.' Bognor looked bothered. A characteristic expression which, unlike others, was entirely revealing about the state of mind behind it.

'There are various possibilities. Either he came about

it honestly or he nicked it. If he nicked it, then why? And for that matter how? If he came about it honestly the implication is that he was there during the bridge.'

Bognor followed this, although with difficulty.

'Let us' – Wartnaby, seeing Bognor's problem, spoke very slowly and distinctly – 'Let us assume that Freddie was there while they were playing. What would he be doing?'

'Mixing the drinks,' said Bognor brightly. 'Busman's holiday. Moonlighting. I can't imagine the Jolly Trencherman pays its barman a great deal. He probably needed the cash.'

'I hadn't thought of that,' confessed Wartnaby. 'Good theory. Perfectly plausible. But I have another.'

'Which is?' Bognor was rather peeved at having his first inspired guess dismissed apparently out of hand.

'Notice,' said Wartnaby, 'that "bridge" has inverted commas round it.'

'So what?' said Bognor. 'Lots of things have inverted commas round them. I don't imagine punctuation was Freddie's strong suit.'

'Sometimes people use inverted commas because whatever is in the inverted commas is code for something else. If you wanted to say *soi-disant* bridge, then you'd put inverted commas round "bridge"! See what I mean?'

'Up to a point,' said Bognor, using the phrase in its Evelyn Waugh/Lord Copper sense. In other words, 'no'.

'Would it be possible that Freddie was there to keep the score?'

'Surely you don't need a scorer for bridge?'

'That,' Wartnaby was clearly nearing the end of his tether, 'is what I'm trying to suggest.'

Bognor shook his head as if trying to rearrange the brain cells. 'I'm sorry,' he said. 'I'm not at my absolute Einstein best this morning.'

'I see that. All I'm suggesting is that this might just be the clue to who killed Freddie.'

'Might it?'

'It might. The 17th of November is only two days ago.

The afternoon of the Artisan Dinner and the day before Freddie was killed. It could well be germane. Anyway, it would be useful to find out.'

'I think it would be suspicious if I went back to Fothergill all of a sudden,' said Bognor. 'And much the same goes for the women. I'll go and see Moulton.'

'Mouldy Moulton,' said Wartnaby. 'I think that's a first-class idea.'

'I suppose I shall have to see him at the brewery.' Bognor shook his head ruefully this time. 'I'm not sure I'm up to the smell of hops and malt or whatever breweries smell of.'

'I'm sure you'll manage.' Wartnaby smiled. 'The other thing is Puce. I'm not necessarily suggesting that Puce is our killer, but, as I've told you, there is very little in Scarpington that doesn't have a Puce finger in it. And that is particularly true of anything to do with the Artisans. So the sooner you fix an interview with him the better.'

'OK,' said Bognor.

Wartnaby looked at his watch. 'I must be off. Don't tell anyone you've seen me. Especially any of my colleagues or there'll be hell to pay. I'm going to lie doggo till breakfast tomorrow. See you then. Toodle pip.'

And with a cheery wave he was gone.

Bognor drank another cup of Wartnaby's Kibo Chagga in a bath which smelt of soapy tangerines. The well-deserved hangover had still not arrived. He missed his wife. On the other hand he couldn't help thinking about the Countess of Scarpington. A pity he had been too drunk to properly appreciate her charms, though he had been alive to the hot and cold sauna and plunge treatment. He winced at the memory. How complicated life was! This wretched business of sudden death dogging his footsteps wherever he went. It was too boring. What was it Monica had quoted at him, oh, yes, 'Do not fear death so much, but rather the inadequate life.' Bertolt Brecht and damn silly if you asked him. Most lives were inadequate. How many people in Scarpington had adequate lives? Not many. You could even argue that it wasn't possible to have an adequate life in Scarpington. What was it those self-satisfied people had said on that irritating radio programme at the end of the week, the one with the very old boring Canadian and the bossy woman who was on TV with Sir Robin Day? The one with the fingernails. Oh yes, was there life after Basingstoke? Or words to that effect. He personally had always had a very good time in Basingstoke, but Scarpington, Scarpington was another ball game altogether.

And what was the significance of the bridge score card? Did Wartnaby know more than he was saying? Was he, Bognor, being really obtuse? Should he ring Parkinson for guidance? Dammit, no. He must use his initiative. It was what he was paid for. Oh why, oh why had he not taken an easy way out when he was a young man? If only he had gone to teach in a prep school and married a matron he could have lived happily ever after. Instead of which here he was banging about the country causing people to drop dead wherever he went. He was beginning to think he was the Angel of Death. After all, there was nothing in the Bible to say what form the Angel of Death should manifest itself in. Wings and a halo? Hardly. Nobody believed that sort of Victorian Enid Blyton mumbo-jumbo any longer. If the Angel of Death were to suddenly manifest himself in England in the late twentieth century, why on earth shouldn't he wear an A and B tie and a tweed jacket? It would be too bloody obvious to have him in chains and a punk haircut with a safety pin through his nose. Or pretending to be a lager lout. Oh God, and now he had to go and see round a brewery where he was going to be as much use as a eunuch in a harem and poor Mouldy Moulton would probably drop stone dead before you could say hop or barley. He sighed out loud and turned the hot tap on with his toe, then couldn't get it off again and had to sit up and turn it with his hand because otherwise he'd be scalded to death and he had no wish to be a down-page paragraph in Harold Fothergill's paper headed 'Board of Trade Investigator boiled to death in bath'.

He sighed again. This wouldn't do. It really wouldn't. He must get on and phone Moulton. One last long wallow. He wished he'd packed the loofah. He must lose some weight, although if he breathed in a couple of times you could almost see ribs. Then like an elderly whale breaking through to the surface he stood, very reluctantly, wrapped a towel round his thickening middle, and went to the bedside phone.

Moulton's secretary was that rare phenomenon – the efficient, polite, on-the-ball personal assistant.

'He's got Mr Batwas Singh from Biotechnology with him,' she said. 'But if it's Board of Trade I'm sure he can be interrupted.'

Seconds later he was through to Moulton. 'Bognor, Moulton here. Heard you were in town. Sorry to miss you at the Artisan dinner. Tragic about poor Brackett. Absolutely tragic. Funeral tomorrow. Said I'd read a lesson and then drinks on the house afterwards. Least I could do. You lunching today? I've nothing on. Pop over about twelvish. We'll arrange a quick spin round the works, then grab a jar and a spot of something in the boardroom. Nothing special, soup and a steak – that sort of thing. Suit you? Good. Terrific. See you at twelve. Look forward to it.'

And that was it. He sounded like a typical King's Scarpingtonian or whatever the school called their alumni. Old Sludgelodes, perhaps.

Bognor dressed. Clean shirt, clean underpants, A and B tie, cavalry twill trousers and the same tweed jacket as yesterday, over which he was relieved, and somewhat surprised, to find he had not been sick.

Then he set about tracking down Puce. This was not as easy. First he rang the local Conservative Association.

'No, I believe Sir Seymour is in London today. You could try his secretary at the House of Commons.'

'No, we're not expecting Sir Seymour today, he's got a pair. He's probably at Puce Investments.'

'I believe Sir Seymour is in Scarpington today. Have you tried Puce International? I'll give you the number.'

'No, he's working from home today. No, I'm afraid I can't

give you the number. No, I can't pass on a message. No, not even for the Board of Trade. And the same to you.'

Bloody woman, said Bognor, crashing the receiver back into its cradle. He picked up the papers that Wartnaby had brought with breakfast. One was the *Scarpington Times*. On the back page it said: 'Botham "no" to Thursday. All-ticket game at the Bog. "Game of two halves" predicts Smith.'

Bognor wondered if Harold Fothergill wrote the headlines. He was not a footy fan and found the ranting purple semi-literacy of most newspaper football reporting no more comprehensible than a computer manual. It appeared that Scarpington Thursday had, for reasons that had something to do with the intervention of Sir Seymour Puce, contrived a friendly match with a team called Lokomotiv Frankfurt. This was not the West but the East German Frankfurt, although Bognor guessed that this had only been realised rather late in the day. He suspected that it had originally been passed off as a considerable coup to get a smart West German team to play what sports reporters always referred to as 'lowly' Scarpington. Now that the Germans turned out to be a ragtag and bobtail collection of part-time Communist lathe operators and tram drivers it was proving difficult to drum up a crowd.

Nevertheless Puce was obviously going to be there. There was a quote from him saying that a man called Gunter Boschmann, the Lokomotiv striker, would walk into the English side if he was English. Bognor sighed and telephoned the Scarpington Thursday ground. At first he got a recorded message advising him of seat availability for tonight's game and for the impending visit of Accrington Stanley next week. He checked the phone book and found another number under 'Administration'. This time, at last, he felt he was getting warmer.

'Sir Seymour is in conference.'

He left his name and said he would be at the Talbot for the next hour or so. Perhaps Sir Seymour would phone back at his convenience. He was keen to make an appointment.

The girl sounded as if she might have scraped a GCSE in

Home Economics. Bognor supposed there was an approximately fifty-fifty chance of the message getting through in an intelligible form.

Bognor sat on the end of the bed and flipped in a desultory fashion at Fothergill's paper. 'Uproar over street sign plan'; 'New Man at the Mosque'; 'Labour lose key ward'; 'Puce unveils expansion plans'; and at the bottom of the front page: 'Top Artisan Dies – "a true son of Scarpington" – Sir Seymour'. Reg did not get a lot of space. 'Mr Reginald Brackett, MBE, Chairman of Bracketts Laundry and Dry Cleaning Services, collapsed and died this week. 56-year-old Mr Brackett was President of the Ancient and Worshipful Scarpington Artisans' Lodge.' Underneath in bold type it said, 'See obituary, page 17.'

Bognor turned to page 17 and saw that Fothergill and Sir Seymour had done poor Brackett proud. There was a picture of him in full Artisan Presidential fig and the headline, 'Scarpington mourns a son' followed by another line which said, 'Reginald Brackett, Laundryman Extraordinary'. Oh, well. There was a very bald summary of what even Brecht would have been pushed to describe as an adequate life and then 'Sir Seymour Puce writes'. Bognor winced. It was clichéd, florid stuff: 'Pillar of the community . . . generous to a fault . . . tireless work for local charities . . . inimitable sense of humour . . . staunchly supported by devoted wife . . . expansive vision of dry cleaning industry . . . keen golfer . . . little-known passion for English folk dances . . . funeral in Artisan Chapel of Scarpington Cathedral'. Alas, poor Brackett, thought Bognor, dust to dust, ashes to ashes and a life reduced to a few column inches of purple and grey by Sir Seymour Puce. Into the archive, into the scrapbook. He supposed he had better try to make the funeral. There was nothing in the piece about 'cause of death'. Natural or induced. Bognor wished he felt nearer a solution. He was learning about Scarpington, all right. Hanky-panky certainly, skulduggery possibly, murder . . . mmmm, not proven, not yet, anyway.

He was about to turn the page when his attention was

caught by another smaller, unillustrated obit. Mr 'Freddie' Grimaldi. Goodness, he thought, 'Grimaldi'. Could the poor barman have been a member of the Monaco Royal House? Why not? A cadet branch, conceived on the wrong side of some half-forgotten historic blanket? 'Mr "Freddie" Grimaldi, who died in a fire at his home in Bloemfontein Gardens, Scarpington, was chief barman at the Talbot Hotel for more than thirty years. He combined a knowledgeable enthusiasm for horse racing with a wide circle of friends. Long one of the city's "characters", he will be much missed. He was unmarried.'

Oh, thought Bognor. Even in death there were relative degrees of adequacy and poor Freddie measured up even less well than Brackett. And what would they say about him when he was dead and gone? 'Simon Bognor who died yesterday led a life unfulfilled . . . witty, handsome, gregarious, his early promise was blighted by a seminal misunderstanding at the Oxford University Appointments Board which led to his appointment as a Special Investigator at the Board of Trade, a position in which he continued throughout his adult life. Stoic and uncomplaining, he nevertheless . . .'

This self-indulgent reverie was interrupted by a summons by telephone bells.

'Bognor,' he said.

'This is Sir Seymour Puce. I'm so glad I caught you.' Bognor stiffened. Not what he had expected. For some reason, the Member for Scarpington was in unctuous mode. Bognor's experience was that most MPs had only two ways of behaving. The creepy treacle which oozed down the line towards him represented one. The other was abrasive mode – spade-calling, unafraid, honest to goodness, man of the people, man of the moment. Bognor found both equally repulsive but was well able to respond in kind.

'Thank you so much for calling back,' he said. 'I know how busy you must be. I wonder if there is the slightest chance I might find a hole in your crowded schedule to have a talk about the place of Scarpington in the, er, British economy with particular relevance to trade, industry and, well, um, life.'

Fifteen all. Sir Seymour slimed back with, 'Perhaps you'd like to join a small party of us at the Lokomotiv Frankfurt game tonight. We'd dine at the ground. I dare say we could find time for a word about Scarpington and the economy. If not we can arrange another meeting. So if you care to present yourself at the Bog around seven o'clock, just ask for me and we'll set you up with a glass of bubbly. Or Old Parsnip, if you prefer. Ha Ha! Is Mrs Bognor still with you? If so, we'd be delighted to see her as well.'

He sounded as if he was reading from autocue.

'I'm afraid,' Bognor couldn't help a little ice creeping into his delivery this time, 'that Monica had to hurry back to London unexpectedly. I'm so sorry. She would have enjoyed it.'

'Never mind,' smoothed the Member. 'I shall look forward to this evening. There'll be a number of Artisans there so you should pick up some useful information quite apart from what I'm able to tell you. So I'll see you at the Bog around seven.'

'I look forward to it,' said Bognor.

'And I also,' concluded Puce in an unusually archaic final smoothness.

What a prat, thought Bognor. He looked at his watch. Time for him to stroll down to Moulton and Bragg. He wondered what he would be able to worm out of Mouldy 'Gus'. He thought back to the piece of paper Wartnaby had salvaged from Freddie Grimaldi's flat: 'Moulton A. 2'. Whatever game the foursome had been playing, Moulton hadn't been much good at it. But then there really wasn't a lot of mileage in being good at bridge. Not in Bognor's book.

CHAPTER SIX

'Beer drinking don't do half the harm of lovemaking' (Eden Phillpotts)

Mouldy Moulton looked like a brewer was supposed to look – a protruding gut, high complexion and mutton-chop whiskers. He would have cut a fine figure in *lederhosen* at the Münchner Oktoberfest with a stein and a sausage.

'Simon Bognor,' he said, rising from behind his desk. 'Jolly d.' He scuttled round and shook hands. From the window they could see the mud-brown Sludgelode rolling turbid towards the sea. Two shaggy shires were plodding in through the gate with a green and grey Moulton and Bragg dray behind them.

'We do things in the old-fashioned way here,' said Moulton. 'Just as we've always done. Water from the Sludgelode or the wells by Sludgelode Fen; our own barley from the family farm at Crankover; cask staves from the Baltic. Moultons have done it like that for hundreds of years.'

'What about biotechnology?' asked Bognor. 'That doesn't sound like a very traditional way of going about things.'

'Ah,' Moulton grinned. 'Batwas Singh, the boffin from Bangladesh. Remarkable chappie, Batwas. Genetic manipulation of yeast is his baby. Don't ask me what it's all about, but it's very much the coming thing. All the big boys are at it. Not necessarily anything to do with beer. He's working on something called, hang on,' he shuffled some papers, 'ah, yes, recombinant serum albumin. It's a burn and shock treatment. You have to diversify to stay alive. Of course the current fad is taking the bloody alcohol out of everything. In the old days we'd have been done under trade description for selling gnat's pee, but now it's all the vogue. Between you and me, I have a plot to market a completely non-alcoholic beer called 'Alte Tästlessche Gnatspee' and pretend it's imported from Dortmund.' He whinnied with mirth, setting his stomach and chins wobbling.

'Now,' he became serious, 'what would you like to do? Quick tour round and then some scoff?'

'Perfect,' said Bognor. 'I just want to get the feel of the place. Nothing too technical.'

Moulton winked. 'Couldn't agree more, old boy. Don't want to get bogged down in a lot of irrelevant detail. It's the broad thrust that counts. We're pretty good on the broad thrust at Moulton and Bragg, I can tell you!'

Bognor agreed that he was a broad thrust person himself.

'I'd show you round *moi-même*,' said Moulton, 'but one or two teensy problems have cropped up, so if you don't mind I'll get our Miss Mimms to whizz you through. She's our head guide and extremely efficient.'

She was, too. It was the full whistlestop, jampacked, twenty-seven new facts a minute number. Miss Mimms was steely grey outside and steely grey within.

'In 1600 there were 46 licensed victuallers in Scarpington, supplying only 1,500 people, but it was not until the Sludge-lode Navigation Act that Josiah Moulton and Ephraim Bragg joined forces to brew Parsnip Ale to a recipe daringly stolen from William Bass of Burton-on-Trent.' Pause two three, smile two three, unspoken 'are you paying proper attention' two three. 'And this is the bottling line all controlled from the computer here which is one of the most sophisticated in the country and has been specially adapted for the new EEC regulation three litre take-home bottle which . . .'

After a while Bognor gave up even the smallest pretence of trying to understand what was going on. Instead he allowed himself to be gently seduced by the mechanical clackety-clack of conveyor belts bumping bottles round the halls;

by the great vats of embryonic lager and porter and Parsnip heaving and pulsating, suppurating and wafting yeasty, hoppish, barleymow smells and flavours around his nostrils; by the clackety-clack of Miss Mimms in her white coat and white hat, reciting facts and statistics and numbers in her flat Scarpington voice; by the sheer, unchanging, mesmerising rhythm of a process which had all the hypnotic qualities of a metronome with the rather awful rider that there were humans in the production line going clackety-clack just like the machines and Miss Mimms's voice. Could you have an adequate life on a production line? At least he only had to watch and nod with simulated interest. Even so Bognor had a feeling that, as far as he was concerned, information itself had strong narcoleptic qualities. As delivered by Miss Mimms, to the accompaniment of updated Japanesed Heath Robinson, it was lethal.

After half an hour, and not a drop to drink, he was unfit to drive. Just about out on his feet.

'You look as if you could do with a stiffener,' said Moulton when Miss Mimms dumped Bognor back in his office.

'Actually, I think I'd better not,' said Bognor. 'I had rather a heavy day yesterday.'

'Didn't we all! Didn't we all!' Moulton rolled his eyes and winked in such a lubricious fashion that Bognor was afraid word had got out about him and the Countess in the sauna. 'What you need is a hair of the dog.'

Bognor forced a laugh. 'I honestly think a low cal lager would be better. Ein Alte Gnatspee, bitte.'

Moulton guffawed back. Bognor could visualise him only too easily slapping his *lederhosen* with a thwack of the hand while yodelling some *mädchen* in a *keller*. Did one yodel *mädchen*? Perhaps not.

'As a matter of fact,' said Moulton, 'we're doing a very hot German trade with our Export Parsnip. Petersilien-wurzel in krautspeak. Bit of a mouthful. But they seem to like it. Petersilienwurzel aus England. Sehr . . . well sehr something or other. Tell you what, why don't we crack a bottle of the Prince of Wales's Parsnip?'

Bognor was now well baffled.

'You what?' he said feebly.

'Old brewing tradition,' said Moulton. 'Every so often we get Royalty to come and mash an alé. The Prince of Wales came and mashed a special Parsnip. It's drinking awfully well.'

Inwardly Bognor groaned, but he judged it impolite to refuse. On his way down to the brewery he had called in at the public library and carried out a quick consultation in the reference section. He was only working on a hunch but, looking at Moulton, he thought it might be worth a try.

'Weak or strong?' he asked.

'Bloody strong!' Moulton winked again. He was winking so much that Bognor wondered if it might be involuntary. He must be careful not to wink back, just in case. 'Take the top of your head off,' said Moulton.

'Sorry, no, I meant cards.' Being deliberately obtuse came easily to Bognor.

'Cards?'

'Weak or strong no trumps.' Bognor hoped he had got it right. His understanding was that this was what a bridge player asked a new partner as they sat down at table for the first time together.

Moulton's appearance conveyed all the mystification that Bognor so often felt on his own account. 'Um,' he said. 'Not with you, old fruit.'

'Fishy one club,' Bognor said. 'Er ... pre-emptive three ...' He hoped he'd read Hoyle's Encyclopaedia of Card Games correctly. 'Bridge,' he went on quickly. 'I'd heard you were into bridge. The Artisan Bridge club. Keen member. You.'

'Ah.' Moulton was pink already, but it seemed to Bognor that this was a pinker shade of pink.

'My mistake. Understood you played in League B. You and Dorothy Brown.'

Oh, aah, and plunge not the finger of enquiry into the pie of impertinence, O my uncle. Moulton was at a serious loss. He had turned into a flobster.

'Sorry,' he said. 'Not with you, my son.'

And at that moment a butler – how ubiquitous was the ersatz butler in middle England – came in with a bottle of the Prince's Parsnip.

'Oh, terrif.,' said Moulton, saved by a suave chap in Moulton and Bragg livery. The salver was silver, the bottle was glass, the label gilded and grand, the effect show-stopping.

Bognor had, in transatlantic idiom, 'intuited' enough to be able to bend and weave. He had, he reckoned, gleaned just enough. Whatever Moulton had been playing at with Mrs Brown, Mrs Festing and Mr Fothergill, it wasn't bridge.

'Gosh, I say,' he said. 'Is this the Prince's Parsnip?'

'Indeed it is.' Moulton may have been aptly named 'Mouldy', but even so he was capable of incisive change of subject. 'Strong, not weak,' he said, meaning the beer, and then booting the unmentionable back into the closet, he added, 'Not much of a one for bridge, to tell the truth. Social obligation, don't you know. Chap has to keep up appearances if only for business's sake. Now, try some of this. I think you'll find it seriously remarkable. Seriously remarkable.'

It was, it was. And, according to Freddie Grimaldi's score card, Moulton had only scored two. But even a rotten bridge player would catch the reference to weak or strong. A rotten bridge player who belonged to a bridge club and played on mid-week afternoons. There was a little mystery here. Another modest Artisan secret. But was it significant? Did it mean anything? Or was it, like so much of the lore and legend of masonic societies, just plain silly?

Moulton smacked his lips. 'Nectar,' he said. 'Pure nectar.'

Bognor smacked his. He felt the beer shoot down his throat and through the complicated apparatus of human plumbing which he could not understand. This beer really did reach parts other things couldn't and it was reaching them at speed. In seconds the alcohol had penetrated the brain and he was half-way back to where he had been the day before. Not yet drunk but scarcely sober.

'Mmmmm,' he said, 'and you're right. Not in the least weak. Very far from gnatspee.'

'About the same strength as sherry.'

After lunch Bognor had to have a bit of a lie-down. Mouldy Moulton was an ass but he was, it seemed to Bognor, a perfectly agreeable ass and harmless. He was also a lavish host, so Bognor was badly in need of bed by three-fifteen when he finally stumbled away from the brewery clutching a souvenir bottle of the Princess's Parsnip (Di had been down to 'mash' a couple of years earlier, though she seemed a less probable beer person than her sister-in-law).

He was just nodding off when there was a knock on the door.

'No, thank you,' he shouted, and turned over, but the knocking persisted. 'Not today, thank you,' he shouted. 'I'll turn the bed down myself. I don't want an After Eight.' This last was a reference to the Jolly Trencherman custom of putting a single After Eight mint chocolate on one's pillow at night. Two in a shared bed. Bognor, who had come across this before, often wondered if it had some sort of sexual connotation but was too embarrassed to ask anyone, even Monica. It was like bidets in the bathroom. He knew they were connected with some sort of deeply personal ablution but was not quite sure exactly what. He couldn't believe the After Eights were just for eating in the conventional way. And was one supposed to do whatever one did with them before cleaning one's teeth? He had been brought up to believe that there was a very precise drill to be followed before going to bed. One folded one's clothes, one put on one's pyjamas, one washed and brushed one's teeth, and one said one's prayers. Then one got into bed and there was no talking after lights out. Any deviation from this and one was beaten. Nothing in his hearty, muscular Christian fee-paying education had prepared him for the mysterious introduction of the After Eight into this ritual.

It was thoughts such as these that kaleidoscoped through what passed for his brain that afternoon as he tried to sleep off the effects of steak, chips and the Prince's Parsnip.

'Go away!' he shouted as the knocking persisted. It was accompanied by a human voice, he now realised, female and familiar.

'Don't be such a bloody oaf,' it was saying. 'It's Diana Scarpington.'

Oh God, he thought, 'unfinished business'. She had come to have her wicked way with him and he was not feeling up to it. Also he was feeling guilty and his wife had walked out on him. This woman was dangerous and must be asked to leave at once.

'Do please go away!' he called. 'You've got me in enough trouble as it is. Go and find someone else.'

'Don't be idiotic. I just want to talk to you.'

'I don't believe you,' he shouted. 'This is very embarrassing. I'm extremely sorry for what happened. I'm afraid I must have had too much to drink.'

'Oh, shut up and let me in. You really are a pompous ass.'

That was the last straw. He was not going to be called pompous by some nymphomaniac jumped-up PR girl. He went to the door, which was chained, and opened it an inch or so.

'You can call me many things,' he said through clenched teeth, 'but not pompous.'

So she laughed at him. 'If you could see yourself,' she said. 'Pomposity incarnate. Let me in.'

'No.'

'Don't be silly. I need to talk to you.'

'You are talking to me.'

'Oh, for God's sake don't be so idiotic. If you go on like this I shall take all my clothes off and say you tried to rape me.'

'You wouldn't.'

'I certainly would.'

Bognor regarded her through the chained gap. She would, too.

He unchained the door. She was wearing a fur, real fur, coat and a similar outfit to the day before, only this time the trousers were tight white and the roll-neck a vivid scarlet.

'You look terrible,' she said. 'I must have been out of my mind.'

'You were drunk.'

'So were you. Anyway, I've always been attracted to unattractive men. Sprockett was pretty repulsive. Anyway, listen, I've found something out. At least I've half found something out. About the Artisans. I thought you might be interested. It's to do with bridge.'

'Uh, uh. Bridge.'

'The Artisans' Bridge Club. It's not bridge they play. Not at all. I thought you ought to know. For your report.'

Bognor raised an eyebrow and did his best to appear quizzical and superior.

'Not bridge.'

'It most certainly is not.'

'Hadn't you better start at the beginning?' he suggested.

She flopped into a Jolly Trencherman armchair mass-produced in some Third World sweat shop by yet another Puce subsidiary.

'Piggy pretended to be cross after you'd gone.'

'So did Monica. Only she wasn't pretending. Thanks to you, she's done a bunk. From now on I'm going to be utterly virtuous.'

'That, you poor mutt, is called shutting the stable door after the horse has bolted. Which in view of the identity of the bolter is rather a good metaphor.'

'That's not funny.'

'No. Sorry. It's not. Anyway, you don't have to worry. I don't fancy you today. Nor it.'

'That's a relief.'

'You've been drinking again.'

'Yes.'

She clicked disapproval. 'Naughty, naughty. Anyway Piggy pretended to be cross. He was a bit cross, but only because the butler had seen. He's very old-fashioned about staff. Minds awfully what butlers see. So I asked what I was supposed to do when he swanned off playing golf. Not, I said, that it made any difference whether he was here or

98

not because as we both knew he was quite incapable of performing the sexual act.'

'Is he?'

'Well, with me, he is. He can't even . . . well there's no need to go into the sordid details. So then he started to get very shirty and I said if he'd been playing golf why wasn't he wet as it had been pouring with rain all afternoon. And then he said he'd been at the Artisans' Bridge Club. And I asked him why, if he were playing cards, he was absolutely reeking of Miss Dior. At which I thought he was going to burst a blood vessel. But all he did was to say in his sniffy House of Lords voice, 'There were ladies present, actually. There are some women who do know how to play cards.'

'You don't play cards?'

'Life's too bloody short.' She snorted. 'But, this is the good bit. Just as I thought he'd calmed down he said that if I must know he'd been having it off with Yvette Sinclair and she had expressed herself well satisfied. Then he went off to his study absolutely blotto and Perkins and I had to undress him and put him to bed.'

'Which equalled the score as far as the butler's concerned.'

She shook her head. 'Not really,' she said. 'Perkins often puts him to bed. But what was interesting was that when we got his shirt off his back was extremely nasty. Badly bruised and cut through the skin in some places. If it was Yvette she must have given him a ferocious going over with a cane or something.'

'Is this Yvette woman something to do with the invalid carriage people?'

The Countess nodded. 'Married to that smarmy Eric. There's something creepy about him. Though I've always thought the creepiest thing about him was his wife. She's a French Canadian.'

'So you think your husband was telling the truth?'

'It explains all that gear he's left in the dungeon. He's always made out it was there "for old time's sake".'

'I noticed,' said Bognor. 'I thought some of it had been used more recently than sixteen hundred.'

'Very observant of you.'

Bognor smiled. 'I'm paid to be observant, my lady.'

'Don't you "my lady" me or I'll start calling you Bognor. You're just like Sprockett in some ways. A massive conceit based on nothing whatever. It must be something they do to boys at Oxford.'

'You never realised your husband was into SM?'

She thought for a moment. 'Now you mention it, I suppose not. I did once bite his ankle by mistake and he asked me to do it again.'

'By mistake? His ankle?'

'Forget it. I was experimenting at the time.'

'So you're telling me your husband spent the afternoon being flagellated at the Artisans' Bridge Club by the French Canadian wife of Scarpington's leading wheel chair manufacturer.'

'Yup.' She smirked and reached into her handbag. From it she produced an Ingersoll key. 'And look what I nicked while he was asleep.'

'Front door key of the Artisans' Bridge Club.'

'Right in one.'

'Do you have the address?'

'It was in his membership book.'

'There's a membership book?'

'Absolutely.'

'Well, this is highly satisfactory. It sounds as if there is more to Artisan bridge than one might think.' Bognor knew he was being pompous. 'It does tend to confirm what I'd been suspecting for quite some time.'

'Oh, yeah.'

'As a matter of fact, oh, yeah.'

She obviously didn't believe him but that didn't matter. She had a key and an address. Bognor, could, he told himself, have found both for himself, given time, but here they were, presented to him on a plate, and an aristocratic one at that. Spode or Crown Derby, as it were.

'Do you think we should check it out?' he asked.

'What do you think?'

'I think, yes.'

'Good,' she said. 'Car's outside, illegal, but I've got a "Doctor" sign which comes in handy.'

It was a white Volkswagen Golf which she drove with the pzazz and chutzpah he would have expected of her. Pedestrians scattered like surprised pheasants in her path.

'Wedgwood Benn Gardens are out beyond the county cricket ground,' she said. 'I guess The Laurels must be one of those late-Victorian numbers built for the younger sons of the fat cats of the Industrial Rev. Know what I mean?'

Bognor knew what she meant.

This was the suburbia of the provincial city, middle England squared. Respectability and substance and not a non-pinko-grey face to be seen anywhere. A Victorian infrastructure with a few knobs on, including, most recently, fibre-glass, white-painted conservatories and satellite dishes. The inhabitants were the heirs of Pooter: 'executives'; computer 'analysts' and 'planners'; representatives; aspiring Artisans all. This was a comfortable world, more comfortable than ever in Thatcher's Britain. Mouldy Moulton wouldn't live here, but his children might and his executives certainly would. The name 'Wedgwood Benn Gardens' had been pasted over the old 'Laburnum Road' when in the Wilsonian sixties there had briefly been a Labour Council in Scarpington. Unlike 'Mandela Road' or 'Brezhnev Place', it had been allowed to stay. This was largely because, like the man himself, 'Wedgwood Benn' had a pleasing anachronistic euphony which fitted in well with the area's bank-managerly Victorianism.

'Here,' Bognor half-remembered some Betjeman, 'a monkey puzzle tree/And there a round geranium bed', Oh yes, and better yet . . .

He chanted aloud

> Each mansion, each new planted pine,
> Each short and ostentatious drive
> Meant Morning Prayer and beef and wine
> And Queen Victoria alive.

'We're here,' said his friend the Countess. 'Wedgwood Benn Gardens. Oh England, my England.'

And there was a monkey puzzle on the front lawn. Not to mention stained glass over the front door and, let into it, the words 'The Laurels'. It was a substantial two-storey pile with dormer windows in the roof and a modest amount of decoration of the curlecued, semi-heraldic, late-nineteenth-century variety. And, oh yes, a shrubbery with laurels.

'Do the Artisans have the whole place?' asked Bognor.

The Countess could not answer. She parked the car a little way down the drive. 'Only one way to find out,' she said.

'What if someone's there?'

'We'll say my husband left something behind and I've come to pick it up.' She smiled sweetly. 'A handkerchief, perhaps. Or something more intimate. Or you can tell the truth. Explain that you're involved in a Board of Trade investigation of the Artisans and you're leaving no stone unturned. Perfectly true.'

'Hmmm.' Bognor was not too sure. Nevertheless, having come this far it would seem cowardly to turn back.

They scrunched up the gravel of the drive which was, indeed, 'short and ostentatious'. It had an 'in' and an 'out' and was obviously stately home derivative, a very very junior version of the great avenues of elms that led from the lodge to the front door of even undistinguished historic houses like the Countess of Scarpington's own.

Alongside the front door there was a brass plaque saying 'Scarpington Artisans' Lodge Clubhouse'.

'I see,' said Bognor. 'Not just bridge. All-purpose. Do you imagine they do lunches?'

'Dunno,' said the Countess. 'It looks as if they should. Piggy's never talked about it, but then he's not as committed to the Artisans as he might be. On account of Puce.'

There was a doorbell, marked, presumably for those of limited intelligence, with the word 'bell'. Bognor hoped Diana Scarpington would press it, but she held back. Not wishing to seem less than adventurous, he pushed.

'It doesn't look as if there's anyone about,' he said, nervously. 'You'd think they'd have some sort of permanent staff, wouldn't you?'

'Not necessarily. If our suspicions are right, they'd hardly want staff cluttering the place up. Staff would sneak. Or try a little blackmail.'

'Maybe,' said Bognor. 'That's what poor little Reg Brackett was attempting when he called on your husband. Incidentally, I can't call him Piggy and I feel I know him too well to call him the Earl. What's his real name?'

'Lionel,' she said. 'But he doesn't like it. Everyone calls him Piggy.'

'Well, I can't,' said Bognor. 'I bet you that's it. Reg Brackett was trying on a bit of blackmail to bail out the laundry and save it from the predatory advances of Mr Clean and Bleach'n'Starch.'

'Pretty silly of him. Piggy hasn't got any money.'

'Reg Brackett wasn't to know that. He knows Lionel married money. He doesn't know you have separate bank accounts and won't give him any of it.'

'I do give him some money,' she objected. 'Ring the bell again. They can't have heard.'

Bognor did as he was told. Force of habit. Even before Monica he had always done what women told him. Mind you, it was his experience that most men did. He was unusual in not pretending otherwise.

'But you'd think twice about giving Lionel hush-money.'

'I most certainly would, but I do wish you'd stop calling him Lionel. His name's Piggy.'

'There's obviously no one in.' Bognor was not going to get embroiled in an argument about the Earl's name. He had observed that he was a porcine figure, overweight with small, bad-tempered eyes, but that was no reason to be gratuitously offensive, even behind his back. Especially behind his back, dammit. Besides, there would be an element of pot calling kettle black if Bognor did call him that. His own eyes were normal size and remarkably good humoured. But he was becoming dangerously close to fat.

'Here's the key,' said Lady Scarpington.

'Are you sure this is wise?' asked Bognor, hesitating.

'Not at all. But I'm determined to see what it is they've been up to.'

'I'm not sure.' Bognor took the key but held it at arm's length as if it might explode on him at any moment. 'Wouldn't it be better to ask someone like Sir Seymour if I could have a look round the Clubhouse? After all, they've got their brass plaque up. They're not trying to conceal anything. It's all above board. Must be. We're obviously barking up the wrong tree.'

'Oh balls, Bognor,' she said, irritably. 'Are you a man or a mouse?'

'Well, since you ask,' he replied, 'there are occasions on which . . .'

'Oh, give it to me,' she said, reaching out a hand.

'No, no,' he said, humiliated, and inserted the key and turned. Bognor had not expected it to be so easy. He had imagined a burglar alarm, or a butler lurking behind a grandfather clock with a blunt instrument. But no. One turn of the key, one gentle push and they were in.

'Shurely shome mishtake!' said Bognor.

'*Au contraire*,' said the Countess.

'I thought we were looking for a cross between the RAC and a brothel.'

'We are,' she said. 'And I think we've found it. This is just front of house.'

Bognor had once, many years ago, played squash with Nigel Dempster at the Royal Automobile Club and although he had never been in a brothel he had a fairly clear idea of what they looked like (a 1950s Indian restaurant face-lifted by Barbara Cartland). The Laurels looked like neither. Institutional, mildly antiseptic, tasteful, impersonal, it reeked of bank managers and bank managers' aunts. In the hall there was a waxed chest of drawers, a grandfather clock, a large arrangement of dried flowers and a portrait of one of Piggy's ancestors by a local disciple of Sir Joshua Reynolds. It was not a good portrait but appropriate.

'Ghastly good taste,' said Bognor.

'Mmmm,' she agreed.

There was a notice board, green felt with a lattice-work of retaining wires for messages and announcements. There was one which said, 'The Funeral service of Reginald Brackett, President, will take place in Saint Cecilia's Cathedral on Friday 20th November. 11.30. Cremation private. Wake, to which all are welcome, at the Goat and Parsnip Brewery, courtesy of Augustus Moulton, Artisan.' Another was a printed card which announced that Mrs Lettice Mildmay, Animal Portraitist, was available for commission. A third said that the Artisans had negotiated a reciprocal arrangement with Der Klub of Frankfurt. Bognor bet that it was the work of Sir Seymour Puce and that he had, once again, got the wrong Frankfurt.

'Dining-room,' hissed Diana Scarpington, who had tiptoed off. 'Do come and look. It's *so* common!'

It seemed perfectly all right to Bognor. A long room with portraits of past presidents round the walls, plus a sort of honours board listing them all. A 'hostess' hot trolley for keeping meals warm sat in one corner. A central table sitting about a dozen was laid as if for dinner and three or four satellites likewise. These were laid for couples and quartets. A serving hatch led through into a kitchen, unmodernised, with a venerable gas-fired range, original sink, a quantity of frayed, soiled dishcloth and a sad smell of fried egg and lard. On the windowsill, one of the oldest packets of Vim that Bognor had ever seen.

On the other side of the entrance hall, a drawing-room or lounge. Comfy chintz chairs, comfy brown carpet, comfy view to monkey puzzle and Wedgwood Benn Gardens beyond, comfy occasional tables, comfy bound copies of *Country Life* and *The Field*.

'Terribly comfy Humphrey,' said Bognor.

The Countess gave him a sharp look. 'What an extraordinarily silly remark,' she said. 'I'm beginning to think you're hopeless. Does your equine wife see the slightest point in you?'

'Don't be so ratty,' he said. 'It *is* comfortable.'

'Those watercolours are quite foul,' said Diana in reply, 'I'll bet they're by . . .' She strained to read the signature. 'Knew it,' she said. 'Nigel Festing's grandmother, Nigella.'

'Who she?' asked Bognor.

'Sometime girlfriend of Gwen John and Violet Trefusis and Vita Sackville-West and anyone else that way inclined,' she said. 'Poet, feminist, occasional lesbian, sort of suffragette, total bore, and, as you can see, perfectly ghastly painter in the tradition of the Edwardian Lady. Yuk. Let's look upstairs.'

There was a loo on the first floor, and a bathroom which raised their hopes. Also a library full of G. A. Henty and Somerville and Ross and R. S. Surtees and other jaunty, nostalgic boys' books. It smelt of cigar. Next door there was a writing room with a view out of the back of the house across suburban garden to the Coke Works and the Victorian grimness of Sinclair's invalid carriage manufactory. And next door to that a bar. Straightforward, masculine, fox-hunting prints and imitation Spy cartoons plus a half-size billiard table and a darts board. Even Bognor had to concede that the darts board was a bit of a lapse.

'It may not be our cup of tea,' he said, 'but you have to admit that there is absolutely nothing here to suggest what we in the trade call "impropriety". Which is to say, "hanky-panky".'

'There's still the attic,' she said. 'Hot air rises; cream comes to the surface; and it's the same with sex.'

'What about your dungeon?'

The question was perfectly fair and she giggled in acknowledgement.

'Come on,' she said. 'That's the exception that proves the rule. I'll bet you anything you like the Artisans have sex in the attic.'

There was another flight of stairs, narrower, meaner, servants – in the old days – for the use of. At the top a door. And on the door, stencilled: 'Bridge Club'.

'Believe that and you'll believe anything,' she said.

'Cynic.' Bognor didn't know what to believe. 'Bet it's locked.'

She turned the handle and pushed. The door opened.

'There you are,' he said. 'If they had anything to hide they'd lock it up.'

'Over-confidence,' she said. 'I'll bet you.'

'You've just got a dirty mind. It's perfectly respectable, honourable, historic, nay . . . oh.'

They had opened the door of the 'Bridge Club'; they had stepped inside; and they now found themselves in what appeared to be some sort of ante-room. There was a corner cupboard, open and full of drink; a sofa and two chairs; a wardrobe. All quite ordinary. The principal decor was not ordinary. It was a mural which covered all the walls and the ceiling. Bognor had only once seen anything remotely like it, and that was in Viscount Weymouth's apartments at Longleat House. The Viscount, a man of parts, had painted what Bognor recalled as a sort of Bayeux Tapestry devoted to copulation. He had never been to India, but he was given to understand that there were temples where something similar went on, where the sex act was depicted in a number of different variations and with no discernible inhibition.

Thus the vestibule of the Bridge Club.

The Countess clapped her hands. 'Oh,' she said. 'How wonderful. It's a Nigella Festing.'

'You're joking,' said Bognor.

'I'm not, I'm not,' she said. 'Oh, do look, the faces are real people. That must be d'eath-Stranglefield. Look at the nose. And surely that is Violet Trefusis – there, dressed as a nun. Well, undressed as a nun if you insist. Oh, what fun. It is, it is. Look – here's the signature.'

And sure enough, there, near the floor in a far corner, was the prim italic autograph she had pointed to in the prim pictures down below. 'Nigella Festing.' And alongside a quotation from Emily Dickinson: 'take all away from me, but leave me Ecstasy.'

'Well, well,' said the Countess of Scarpington. 'Randy old bat!'

'Are you sure?'

'Absolutely. And she died during the war, so this whole charade must have been going on for ages. What a lark! Jolly inventive, too. Look at these two. I don't actually think that's physically possible. You'd need to be at least triple jointed and as for that one over there, that is not only impossible but downright degrading.'

'Is it supposed to be the Garden of Eden?' asked Bognor. 'This looks like a serpent.'

'Translated to Scarpington. Look, that's the Castle and there's the King's School and Sludgelode Fen and the Brewery. It's wonderful.'

'And proof positive of something rotten in the state of Scarpington.'

'Well, it is rather.' She giggled. 'We've still got some exploring to do.'

There were three doors off the room of the Nigella Festing murals. Bognor opened the first.

'Aha,' he said. 'Not much doubt now.'

It was a simple room. That is to say, it was plainly furnished with none of the frills and ruches and tucks and other flummery that Bognor vaguely associated with this sort of riggish bawdry. But there was no disguising its essential purpose. All four walls and the ceiling were covered in reflecting glass. The carpet was black and so was the bed which was made with black sheets and black pillow cases. The bed, a king-size, was the only item of furniture.

Diana Scarpington sat down on it and the whole thing wobbled like blancmange or a volatile Connemara peat bog Bognor had once encountered.

'Waterbed,' she said. 'Oh, very sixties. Very Carnaby Street.'

Bognor led the way out of this room and through one of the other two doors. This room was identical except that the colour was gold – carpet, bed, sheets and pillow cases, all gold. This bed was also king-size and water-filled.

'So what are the secrets of the third room?' asked Bognor.

'Can't you guess?' asked the Countess. 'I'm damned sure I can.'

They entered. It was a much smaller room with two functional chairs behind two functional tables, on one of which there was a TV set plus video with a large number of cassettes. Each table had an angle-poise lamp. The walls of this room were also covered in a glassy substance but it did not reflect. Far from it. These walls were transparent.

'Hang on.' The Countess tripped out and switched on lights in the gold and black bedrooms, then came back to the small room with the video and switched off the overhead light and turned on the two angle-poises.

'Oh, I see,' said Bognor. And did, too. Both bedrooms were now clearly visible.

'Neat, eh?' she said. 'Custom built for the voyeur.' There were two pads of familiar lined paper on the table-tops.

'Not just for voyeurs,' said Bognor. 'There is a serious kink in all this.'

'What do you mean?'

Bognor told her about the 'bridge' score card that Wartnaby had conjured from Freddie's flat. He did not say where or how he had been shown it, only that he had seen a score card for an alleged Division B of the Artisans' Bridge League with a two for Gus Moulton, a three for Dorothy Brown, a seven for Angela Festing and a nine for Harold Fothergill.

'Oh ho!' said Diana Scarpington, eyes revolving with genuine surprise for once. 'League sex. What a brill idea! You could patent that and make a fortune.'

'Come on,' said Bognor. 'Not in the Age of Aids.'

'Oh, I don't know,' she said. 'They're obviously very fussy about who joins in.'

'And you'd no idea?' he asked.

'None. I suppose Piggy thought I wouldn't approve. Or maybe he didn't like the idea of sharing me around. Can't say I'd fancy some of the members. Ugh!'

'He probably thought you were a bit out of their class.

You'd be too good for them. Like asking Scarpington Thursday to play Liverpool.'

'Careful,' she said, and then, 'Shhh. There's someone coming.'

She had heard a creak on the stair. No question. It was a definite footstep. And another. And another. Purposeful, self-assured. An Artisan, thought Bognor, coming for a rubber of bridge. And then the sound of a second pair of feet. The first male; the second female. And voices. Conversation.

'Oh, hello, Edna, long time no see. We're in "gold" this evening aren't we?'

'So I believe. I'm a bit out of practice, I'm afraid, Nigel. Relegated from League B. And, of course, you've just come up from D. Mind you, I'm not too sure about some of the marking recently. I only got a three for my match with Stan and I thought I was worth at least a five. He thought so too. I always felt there was something not quite right about the way Grimaldi scored.'

'Poor Grimaldi.'

'Yes. Not that I ever liked him. He set fire to himself, didn't he?'

'Something like that. Drunk, I suppose. Who's scoring tonight?'

'Not sure,' said Nigel. 'We're early. Talking of drink, do you fancy one? Get you in the mood.'

'We're not really supposed to until the scorer gets here. Or scorers.'

Nigel gave a short, sharp laugh. 'They don't seem too worried about that these days. Provided we don't take anything off. One or two of the scorers seem to set an increasing amount of store by the strip. I personally think it should be discounted altogether. Call me old-fashioned if you will, but that's my view. And I do think they should seriously consider introducing a handicap system. Some of the younger members are operating under a distinct advantage which has nothing to do with skill.'

Even the Countess of Scarpington was beginning to show

signs of embarrassment at overhearing this exchange. Bognor was scarlet.

'I think we should confront them,' he said. 'We're going to be discovered soon enough anyway.'

'Oh, God!' she whispered back. 'Nigel Festing is such a little wimp. And Edna Fothergill. Edna Fothergill . . . the very thought of the two of them together on a gilt waterbed. And being assessed. I can't bear it. It's too too much.' It would be overstating it to say that she was torn between tears and laughter, but she was having trouble in deciding whether it was all too too terribly sad or too too terribly funny. On balance, as usual with her, comedy prevailed over tragedy. In any case, when she said something was sad she used the word in a disdainful, pejorative sense. As far as Diana Scarpington was concerned, to say that something was 'sad' meant that it was lacking in style or chic. It was an essential strength and weakness in her character that she was scarcely capable of appreciating the word in its true sense. She was one of life's true flippants.

'There's no alternative,' he said. 'We have to reveal ourselves.'

'OK,' she said. 'Lead on.'

And for once he did.

'Mrs Fothergill,' he said, advancing into the room of Nigella Festing's naughty murals, 'Simon Bognor. We spoke after the dinner the other night. Your husband (Oh God, he had not meant to put such a heavy emphasis on the word "husband") was kind enough to buy me a pint of Parsnip in the St Moritz.'

'Oh, Mr Bognor,' Edna Fothergill simpered. 'Fancy finding you here. Are you taking part or scoring? And Diana, I rather thought Lionel wasn't keen on your joining in the "bridge". Has he relented? What fun! How nice.'

Bognor was somewhat taken aback by this response. He had anticipated the guilty confusion that he himself had experienced on being caught in semi-flagrante in the sauna. Mens sauna in corpore . . . no, no, he told himself. Take a grip.

'I'm afraid,' he said, in the icy tones of a senior Board of Trade investigator, investigating, 'that the Countess and I are not here to participate or adjudicate.'

'Piggy left a pair of socks behind last time he was in,' said the Countess. 'I said I'd drop by and pick them up.' She smiled.

'I don't believe we've had the pleasure.' Nigel Festing put down what looked like gin and tonic and solemnly extended a hand, which, to his mild chagrin, Bognor took and shook. 'Nigel Festing,' said Nigel Festing.

'Simon Bognor,' said Simon.

There was one of those pauses. Pretty pregnant. Which in the circumstances was understandable.

'I understand,' said Bognor, 'that these er . . . interesting . . . murals are the work of your grandmother.'

'Oh, how clever of you to spot it,' said Nigel. 'Not her usual style, of course. There are some watercolours in the drawing-room which are rather more typical. But she did experiment in the, um, erotic vein. We have some peculiarly fine notebooks of hers at home. Fine, fine work. But a little strong for popular taste.'

'Excuse me just one moment,' said Edna Fothergill. She simpered again. 'Must powder my nose.'

'Look,' said Bognor, when Mrs Fothergill had left, 'I'm not here to make moral judgements.'

'Oh, quite,' said Festing. 'Absolutely. I do so very much agree. Not a moral issue. That's the whole essence of the Artisan Understanding. With respect, Diana.'

'I'm here on behalf of the Board of Trade.' Bognor was anxious to retain control of the situation.

'The Great Architect of the Universe would understand that, Mr Bognor.'

'Isn't that a Masonic phrase?'

'We have some affinity with the Masons,' said Festing.

'But you're sexier?'

A thin smile. 'So we've always thought.'

'Look,' – Bognor could smile as thin as the next man – 'I said I don't want to push the moral thing, but the fact is that you're really just running a wife-swapping thingy under the pretext of a sort of Rotary Bridge Club.'

'So?'

This was a stumper. Bognor hadn't thought it through.

'I have a friend,' he said, 'called Molly Mortimer on the *Globe*. If she knew about this she'd have a field day.'

'So would we. Put up a class silk like "Noisy" Simpson and we'd clean up. We're not doing anything illegal. I should know. Festing, Festing, Hackett, Festing and Festing have been interpreting the law since the law began. Practically speaking. I am the senior partner. Frankly, what I don't know about the law isn't worth knowing.'

'Look,' Bognor made as if to put his cards on the table, 'two men have died in the last forty-eight hours. Both were connected with your "bridge" club.'

'So?' Festing had an obvious capacity for truculence. 'Poor Reg had a heart attack. Public speaking always had a terror for him. Bang! Woof! Over he keels and dies in the small hours in Scarpington General with the good wife holding his hand. As for "Freddie" Grimaldi, he set fire to a foam-filled piece of upholstery while under the influence. Happens to the best of us. And to the worst, which was him.'

Bognor decided to get heavy.

'If your clients,' he said, 'were to realise that you were given to cavorting about on a golden waterbed with the likes of Edna Fothergill there might be, how shall we say, at least a marginal decline in enthusiasm for your practical advice. And if I were to extend that particular piece of observation I dare say I could blow a sizeable hole in the side of the Scarpington economy. What price Moulton and Bragg's Old Parsnip if the punters thought it had been brewed by a sex maniac? Who'd buy a Sinclair invalid carriage if they thought the manufacturer was bouncing about on a waterbed in Wedgwood Benn Gardens with the local dairyman's doxy?'

'The Artisans have been behaving thus for ever,' said Festing. Very sententious.

'Antiquity will get you nowhere,' said Bognor. 'You Scarpingtonians are sex mad, and it won't do. It really won't.'

'Nigel,' – Diana Scarpington's smile was clearly intended to defuse a situation which was growing ever more awkward – 'as Simon said, we're not here to strike moral attitudes. In my case I am simply curious. My husband has never so much as mentioned any of this to me and as a wife I have a natural curiosity. For example, most wives seem to be asked to become members. One can't help feeling a little left out.'

'I'm afraid, Diana, that divorced wives are unacceptable to Artisans. At least when it comes to carnal knowledge within the Bridge Club.' He said this with a stiff distaste as if he had a mouth full of prune. 'The Great Architect is very precise on that point.'

From downstairs came the sound of speech. It was Edna Fothergill talking into thin air.

'Oh hell,' said the Countess. 'Is that silly cow on the phone? I thought "call of nature" meant something quite different.'

'Warning off the other players?' Bognor did his best to glare at Festing.

'And the umpires, or scorers or whatever?' Diana Scarpington could look frostier than Bognor. Festing quailed visibly.

'*Tant pis*,' she said. 'Now that we've got this nasty little man here we can at least ask some questions.'

'I'm not obliged to say anything. Anything at all.' Festing had taken on a hunted look. Bognor sensed he was bulliable, but at his most dangerous when physically threatened.

'Look,' said Bognor. 'Be reasonable. I'm certainly not here to intrude into private grief. If, as you say, there is nothing illegal in it then you have nothing to hide.'

'That,' said Festing, 'is a complete *non sequitur*.'

'Maybe. I'm not a lawyer.' Bognor sat on the sofa and sighed. 'I am simply here to find out what makes the Scarpington business community, er, tick. I'm not in the name-calling business. I am neither a journalist nor a police-man. I am, as I have told you, a Special Investigator for the Board of Trade.'

'That could mean anything.'

'As such,' – Bognor was not going to respond to cheap lawyer's gibes – 'it would help me to know a little more about the activities of the Bridge Section of the Artisans' Lodge. If only in order to be able to dismiss it from my report. Which, in any case, is an internal government matter and as such confidential. Highly confidential. Which is to say, top secret. Anyone divulging anything in it to a member of the press or the public would go directly to gaol without, as it were, passing "Go". So your secrets are safe with me. On the other hand, if you choose to be obstructive it is within my compass to make life exceedingly difficult for you. Which I should not like.' He paused. 'And nor would you.'

'What do you want to know?' Festing took a silver cigarette case from his pocket and lit an untipped Navy Cut.

'Well, for a start, how long has all this been going on?'

'It was an ancestor of her husband's who started it all. "Black Jack Stranglefield", the fourth Earl. He was a rake.'

Bognor, losing concentration momentarily, had a sudden and bizarre horticultural image conjured up for him.

'As in rakehell,' said Bognor, 'loose-fish, rip or whore-monger?'

Festing regarded him with newly awakened curiosity.

'He had more than an eye for the girls. In fact he was said to be the last nobleman in England to exercise the *droit de seigneur*. He was a Hawcubite and a founder member of the Hellfire Club. When he succeeded his father as Grand Patron of the Artisans he, well, he made a number of changes.'

'Like what?'

'Don't be obtuse, Diana. He introduced a sexual dimen-sion, which as far as I can see from reading between the lines of the old minute books consisted entirely of his having his way with the members' wives. But in the nineteenth century it got democratised.'

'So,' said Bognor, 'that everyone was allowed to have his way with the members' wives?'

'That's an exceptionally vulgar way of putting it, Mr Bognor.'

'But true.'

Festing did not disagree. Edna Fothergill returned to the room. She appeared mildly distrait but sat down on a chair and tried to compose herself. Bognor glanced in her direction and attempted to curl his lip. But without a lot of success.

'And now it's become competitive.'

'A benefit of Thatcherism,' said Festing. 'We'd had enough of the old sixties *laissez-faire* rubbish. Frankly, the Bridge Section had degenerated into nothing more than a whole lot of people simply sleeping around. So one or two of us got together and completely revitalised it. We gave it a new sense of purpose.'

'A league system.'

'Absolutely.' A gleam of fanaticism had appeared in the little lawyer's eyes. 'It's just like my squash club. Only you have to have a judging system, so in that sense it's more like dressage or figure skating. Everyone gets marked out of ten but the rules are all clearly understood. You get points under a whole lot of different headings like enthusiasm and effort and innovation.'

'And politeness,' said Edna.

'And politeness,' confirmed Festing. 'We're very hot on etiquette and good manners. Pleases and thank yous do matter. So each league is four people.'

'Opposite sexes?' This from the Countess.

'We have had some trouble from the gay community over this, but at the moment we're being rigorously convention-al. Each league is four, so everyone plays two matches per session and then the winner goes up a division and the loser down.'

'And I dare say you present a cup to the overall champion at the end of the year.'

'As a matter of fact, yes.' Festing seemed quite cross at the ironic tone of Bognor's question.

'And you probably have an annual knock-out competition too?'

'And what's so funny about that?' Festing was much affronted. 'The d'eath-Stranglefield Bridge Cup. Your husband donated it, Diana. It's a very handsome trophy.'

'Bet he's never won it,' said the Countess.

'And all Artisans belong?' asked Bognor.

'Technically speaking,' said Festing, 'an Artisan may opt out. Like being a conscientious objector. But it's very seldom done. Not the thing. Un-Scarpingtonian. Not Artisan.'

'And you mustn't think,' said Edna Fothergill, 'that any Tom, Dick or Harry can become an Artisan. The entry requirements are extremely stiff.'

'I thought,' said Bognor, 'that it was all to do with old boy networks and business proficiency.'

'Dear me, no.' Edna Fothergill's expression had taken on an alarming, almost evangelical fervour. 'Every candidate has to come here to be examined.'

'Goodness,' said Bognor. 'And who does the examining?'

Festing chipped in quickly. 'It would be grossly improper for us to divulge such a thing,' he said. 'It would be quite contrary to every conceivable Artisan Understanding, written and unwritten.'

'But Nigel, dear,' said Edna. 'It can't possibly matter to poor Reg and Freddie Grimaldi. They're both dead.'

CHAPTER SEVEN

A Game of Two Halves

The Bog was not one of the country's great football grounds.

That, however, was very far from being the whole story. In 1893 when Scarpington Thursday first joined the league and the Crankover Colliery was in full production and the antimacassar factory had not gone bust and the Etna match factory had not burned down and when Sinclair's and Moulton's employed more men than machines, then tens of thousands had crammed into the Bog to see Thursday play the likes of Preston North End and Bolton Wanderers and Blackburn Rovers. They had stood at the Sludgelode End in their flat caps and shapeless coats and they had understood the game and appreciated its finer points and even applauded the opposition. If you believed old men in their cups, some of them had even worn clogs.

Men had been men then. The early managers of Scarpington Thursday had only to go to the mine and whistle, and up came another of the burly, baggy-shorted, Brylcreem-slicked centre forwards for whom the team was famous. Men like 'Slogger' Harris or 'Titch' Nisborne or Alf Hattersley, the man they called 'the Wizard'. Scarpington Thursday had been a name to conjure with in those days. They had gone to Wembley. Scarpington men had played for England. Wherever a Scarpington man travelled in the civilised world strangers would nod respectfully when the town was mentioned and they would say 'Ah, Scarpington Thursday!' with a voice full of something not far short of awe.

Then the lean times had come to the town and to the club.

Thursday plummeted downwards until one dreadful season when they finished at the very bottom of Division Three North. The old stands mouldered and festered and crumbled and rotted and rusted until the one at the Sludgelode End was condemned as unsafe and had to be demolished, leaving only an empty uncovered terrace of concrete steps. The huge crowds drifted away and went to bingo instead. Or stayed at home to watch the telly. Those few who did come only came for the fighting and the drinking and the being sick and the chanting of 'Out, out, out' at the board of directors, presided over for too many years by Nigel Festing's father, the late and unlamented Alderman Festing.

And finally there had been a revolution, not unlike that which overtook the Bridge Section of the Artisans. Out went fusty, crusty old Festing and his musty board and in came thrusting, dynamic, trendy, cigar-smoking, velvet-collared, entrepreneurial, Thatcherite, you've guessed it, Sir Seymour Puce. A stealthy buying of the old farthing shares, a vulpine swoop at the AGM, a couple of well-concealed and tellingly aimed stabs in the back and the deed was done.

That was five years ago. Since then there had been three new managers and a number of expensive and not wholly unsuccessful signings of players. The team had risen. Not all that far, and not as far as Sir Seymour would have wished, but it had risen. There had been ugly rumours that he was to sell the Bog for an office development. Harold Fothergill, in an uncharacteristic fit of insubordination, had run a *Times* campaign and had thousands of 'Save the Bog!' car stickers printed. The scheme had been quietly shelved and Sir Seymour had, instead, devoted his energies and money into turning the Bog into 'the finest stadium in the land' with a 'brand new leisure complex' and 'Megastore' on the waste land behind the Sludgelode End stand, now rebuilt and named, in an ironic tribute, 'The Alderman Festing Stand'. It was actually a cheapskate effort and used mainly by visiting fans. The smart stand, the one with the directors' box and the 'corporate entertainment' boxes occupied by companies like Sinclair's and Moulton and Bragg, was what had once been the 'East' Stand and was now, of course, 'The Puce'.

It was at the private directors' entrance to this magnificent monument of glass and concrete that Bognor's taxi dropped him half an hour before the kick-off against Lokomotiv Frankfurt.

His head was still spinning, partly from the effects of lunch, following on the disasters of the previous day and partly from the enormity of the revelations at The Laurels. They bothered him. Part of his botherment was sheer shock. He simply had not expected to find such a thing happening in middle England. He remembered a school history master returning from jury service with scandalous tales of incest and perversion in rural Dorset, but at the time he had discounted them as the product of a fevered imagination and a desire to shock or titillate small boys. He knew from his occasional furtive glimpses of the tabloid press and from page three of the *Daily Telegraph* that naughty things did go on behind the curtains of apparently respectable homes, but he always supposed that they were exceptional and that chastity or at least a decently abstemious monogamy such as that practised by himself and his own dear wife was the rule. And now this. He regarded himself as a man of the world who had knocked about and seen a thing or two and was no saint himself, but even so he had to admit that, to his surprise, he was, well, in a word, shocked. It was the only word for it.

He knew that he must dismiss the notion immediately. It was no part of his job to be upset by such things. 'Shock' should simply not be a word in the Board of Trade lexicon. Nevertheless he had to confess that try as he might the shock lurked. It was a nuisance and he must do his best to ignore it, but it could only fog his otherwise clear vision and penetrating analytical powers. That and the Old Parsnip.

The trouble was that he was finding it difficult to decide on its relevance. Was the private life of the Artisan members and their wives relevant to his professional enquiries? There was, after all, a right to privacy. Or should be. But could an entire business community be said to have a private life or to enjoy the privilege of avoiding the inquisitorial searchlight of a government investigator? He rather thought not. If this was how middle England behaved, then the people had a right to know. Well, Parkinson had a right to know, which was perhaps not quite the same thing. It would have to go into his report. He had no alternative.

Then there was the question of the deaths. What of them? Was the odious little Festing creature correct in saying that there was no connection between this amateur vice ring and the sudden demise of two of its leading arbitrators? Well, maybe. Wartnaby had said nothing about the post-mortem on Brackett, so Bognor could not yet say whether it had been natural causes or not. It would be next to impossible to prove that the Grimaldi business was not a case of auto-combustion. And if the Chief Constable really was in the Artisan pocket, as Wartnaby suggested, then there wasn't a chance in hell.

This was the year of the inflatables in football. Blow-up bananas in Manchester, balloonic haddocks in Grimsby, gaseous bees from Brentford and in Scarpington buns. After a particularly inept performance Radio Scarpington had described the team as having played 'like a load of cream puffs'. Hence inflatable chocolate éclairs.

There were already a few of them huddled together on the terraces of the North Stand when Bognor arrived. Some of their owners were even trying to beat the drizzle with a dirge-like version of 'Puff the Magic Dragon'. The combination of bedraggled provincial punk, jaunty sad song and bobbing brown and cream prophylactics was not encouraging.

The part of the stadium in which Bognor found himself was quite different – expensive rubber plant, thick pile carpet and a poster saying that the guest artiste at the annual Directors' Dinner Dance would be 'Dr Mel Henry and the Consultants'. There was a photograph, presumably of the doctor, who appeared to be playing a trombone in the French Quarter of New Orleans.

'Sir Seymour is expecting you,' said the girl at the desk.

She was blonde, pneumatic, marginally alluring, crisply turned out, but in a sense that Bognor was unable to define with real precision she was last year's model. He supposed that was the difference between Scarpington and the Big Smoke. Even in the age of the fax, the modem, the dish and Sky TV the message took time to get through. The Tottenham Hotspur girl of today was the Scarpington Thursday girl of tomorrow. In metropolitan terms this was little Miss Yesterday.

'Good of you to come, Mr Bognor. Or Simon, if I may.'

Sir Seymour was standing on the ankle-high Wilton substitute (manufactured by Puce Industries of Taiwan) which covered the area immediately outside the lift at boardroom level. Immediately behind him was the famous picture of the Alf Hattersley goal which knocked Arsenal out of the Cup one dazzling January Saturday in the early nineteen-thirties.

'Very good of you to ask me, Sir Seymour,' said Bognor, wondering how it was possible for a man to exude quite such an air of prosperity. It was one thing to wear a tailored suit from Savile Row and hand-made shoes from Mr Lobb and a Hilditch and Key shirt and a Turnbull and Asser tie and to be waving a zeppelin of a Havana from Davidoff and to stink of Penhaligon's Hamman after-shave, but for all these things to coalesce into a sort of second skin was quite another. The second you saw him you knew that Puce was prosperity made flesh, the very incarnation of wealth, a man for whom, in the beginning, the blank cheque was God.

'Always glad to see a man from the Board of Trade,' said Sir Seymour with about as much conviction as a damp squid. '"No nation was ever ruined by trade." Benjamin Franklin said that, as I expect you know, Simon. I meet a lot of prejudice against trade and commerce. Meet it wherever I go, most of all in the Palace of Westminster. The Americans have a proper respect for trade. The British seem not to. We're a workshy nation. Or were until Mrs Thatcher, God bless her. But to listen to some of those ginger-bearded, sandal-wearing, nut-cutlet-eating *Guardian* readers in the

House of Commons you'd think an honest day's work was an offence against nature. The university lecturers are the worst. Load of pinkoes. I'd close the lot, if I had my way. Including Oxford. Come and have a drink. What's your poison?'

Bognor blenched. Was it his imagination, or did they drink rather a lot in Scarpington? Mrs Currie, once Minister for Personal Hygiene and Eating Habits, had intimated that people from north of the Watford Gap drank too much, though Bognor had always put the remark down to prejudice. Maybe she was right.

'I don't know,' said Sir Seymour, ushering him through a door to their right, 'if you've tried our famous Old Parsnip. It's one of Scarpington's many contributions to world civilisation.'

Bognor quailed again.

'I think—' he said, but was not allowed to finish.

'Freddie Grimaldi, the barman at the St Moritz who passed on so tragically the day before yesterday, used to mix something called a Scarpington Special,' Puce sighed, 'but the secret died with him. Now, allow me to effect some introductions.'

There had obviously been a three-line whip of Artisans and Artisan hangers-on and supporters. Even Piggy, the Earl, was there. Bognor and he shook hands with an icy stiffness which Bognor felt everyone present must have sensed. Then he was passed to the Bishop who muttered something incomprehensible in what could well have been Latin. Then Harold Fothergill.

A white-jacketed waiter loomed bearing a pint of beer on a tray.

'Aha, Parsnip,' said the MP. 'I think you'll be amused by Parsnip's presumptions.' And he laughed, chins a-tremble.

'I thought you did poor Brackett proud,' said Bognor. 'Mrs Fothergill must have been pleased.'

Why was he talking like this? It must be the alcohol, the lack of Monica, shyness, strange surroundings.

'We try to speak well of the dead,' said Fothergill. 'Not like your so-called "national" newspapers.'

Bognor had to say a silent *touché* to this. He had personally witnessed the cut-throat competition between the obituary staffs of the rival London dailies. Ambulance-chasing to the morgue and beyond. Character assassination of the corpse. For once, in the provinces, a gentler, kinder, more agreeably hypocritical attitude prevailed toward the dead. 'Bloody rude' was still euphemised into 'always spoke his mind' or 'no sufferer of fools'; 'crashing bore' became 'noted for his keen sense of humour' or 'life and soul of the party'; even Alderman Festing was said, in the *Scarpington Times*, to have been 'much loved'. London papers, in comparison, though nervous, for reasons of libel, about kicking a man when he was down were positively gleeful about kicking him when he was dead.

'Speaking of Mrs Fothergill,' said Bognor, with metropolitan malice, 'she not here?'

'She has a bridge evening,' said Fothergill, and for a second their eyes engaged. 'Edna's never been much of a one for football, I'm afraid.'

'Ah,' said Bognor. 'I see. You not a bridge player?'

'It's a league foursome,' he said. 'We don't play as husband and wife. In fact, between you and me that's considered not befitting an Artisan. You're allowed to play with one another's partners but not one's own.'

'Sounds rather risqué.' Bognor smiled over the froth of his Parsnip and had the satisfaction of drawing blood. Not a lot, for in truth Harold was an etiolated, bloodless being. In the old days editors had been different. Today it was computer skills, marketing and man-management that got them where they were, not booze and scoops.

'Keen on soccer?' asked Puce, who did not seem over-keen on too much talk of bridge. 'Fundamental to the life blood of the city. With respect to his Grace, this club is more central to the community than the cathedral ever was or will be.'

Puce never waited for an answer, Bognor observed. Sure sign of success. He looked out through the plate glass to the bobbing inflatable éclairs and wondered if Puce was right.

'I was at a rugger school,' said Bognor, 'so . . .'

'Ah, a rugger bugger, eh!' Not only did Puce not let you answer his questions, he didn't allow you to finish your own. 'Well, Scarpington's a soccer town. Ha!' This last was not so much a laugh as a seal's bark, a piece of verbal punctuation.

'I . . .' ventured Bognor, without real optimism. He was duly drowned in more Puce verbiage.

'Simon here,' and he smiled without warmth or affection at the Editor of the *Times*, 'has come here to see what makes this town tick. So what better place could we bring him than to the Bog?'

'You should understand by now,' said Fothergill, toadying into the tiny gap left by Puce's pause for a sip of his drink, 'that what makes Scarpington tick above all else is Sir Seymour Puce and all his works.' He simpered.

Sir Seymour resurfaced, not looking too pleased. There was, his expression seemed to say, sycophancy and there was sycophancy. It could be overdone.

'Tonight, Simon,' he said, 'is a fine example of what can be achieved in a place like this, at a time like this, by people like us. Here we are in Scarpington playing games with our brothers from the East German Republic in a spirit of amity and friendship. It is thus that we foster fraternal relations and, not to put too fine a point on it, trade. Because of initiatives such as this the invalid carriages of Scarpington will be crossing the Elbe; the Old Parsnip of Scarpington will flow from West to East; even Harold will speak peace unto nations. We do have the top banana of the local Zeitung here, don't we Harold?'

'None of the krauts seem to have arrived yet. They're supposed to be coming in a charabanc from the Talbot.' Fothergill sighed. 'I'm not at all sure about my opposite number. Obviously a keen party member. Not much humour and his English isn't up to much either.'

'How's your German?' asked Bognor.

Fothergill looked as if he might do Simon serious damage, but at that moment the door burst open and with a cry of 'Achtung! Achtung!' from Sir Seymour a bus-load of Lokomotiv hangers-on debouched into the board entertainment lounge.

They looked, at first glance, disturbingly like their Scarpington oppos. Perhaps, thought Bognor, small-town success is the same under both systems. Maybe the Mayor and the Editor of the Paper and the Boss of the Factory and of the Brewery were the same in both places.

And, lo, just to emphasise this point who should heave into view but his lunchtime host, the jovial bonhomous Mouldy Moulton, and who should he have in tow but a tubby chap with a paunch straining over his mass-produced people's trousers. Mouldy introduced him as 'Herr Doktor Gottlieb who brews the official state pilsner in his part of the world'. Puce sidled off to circulate and they were joined by a thin, pallid, intense man with wire-rimmed spectacles of a sort not much seen in the West since 1914. If ever. 'And this,' said Harold Fothergill, 'is Herr Doktor Schubert, Editor of *The Frankfurter*. At least I think he said it was just called *The Frankfurter*. Ist das richtig, Doktor Schubert?'

Doktor Schubert smiled, revealing an impressive quantity of gold tooth, and said, 'How do you do. I am very pleased to be in your so beautiful country. I bring fraternal greetings from the People's Democratic Public of Germany. Please.' And he shook hands all round, inclining his head with a sharp snap every time he did so. Then he shut up. Bognor guessed that that was the end of his English and that he would not speak again.

'Back on the beer, eh?' said Moulton. He was drinking pink gin. Or rather he had just finished a pink gin and asked a waitress to fetch him 'a double Gordon's with a splash of Malvern Water, thanks ever so much, darling'.

'No choice in the matter.' Bognor swayed gently. 'Sir Seymour insisted.'

'Ah.' Moulton turned to Doktor Gottlieb. 'I was explaining to Franz here that Sir Seymour was the Führer of Scarpington. Or the Gauleiter. Perhaps that would be more appropriate. I'm not too hot on what they have in the iron curtain bit of Deutschland.'

Franz was obviously a bit of a card. He also gave every indication of having had a few Parsnips. 'In my country we are all sehr democratic being but I think we also are having our how do you say Sir Seymour Puce. Your British beer also is good but your Parsnip is best.' He raised his glass. 'Heil Parsnip!' he said, and they all raised their glasses and said 'Heil Parsnip'.

'You are from the State Polizei. Gus is telling me,' Doktor Gottlieb was all amiable curiosity, 'you do not seem like our German policemen.'

'Well,' said Bognor, 'I'm not really a policeman as such. I'm what's called a Special Investigator of the Board of Trade.'

'How do you say, "investigator"?'

'Sort of detective,' said Moulton. 'Finds things out.'

'Ach so', said Franz. 'I am correct. You are detective. Margery Allingham, Dorothy Sayers, P. D. James, Ruth Rendell. Everyone in Germany now is reading the famous English detective stories. You are just like Lord Peter Wimsey.'

'Well, no, I, er . . .' Bognor had often thought of himself in very much the same terms as the cricket-playing, aristocratic, Balliol-educated sleuth who was so much more devilishly brilliant than he allowed himself to appear. But he had never dared articulate the idea even to Monica. Well, most of all to Monica. He must stop thinking of her. He was missing her. Damn.

'So,' Franz said. 'You are looking for bodies, yes?'

'We've got plenty of those, Franz, old fruit. Running at the rate of one a day practically.'

The German's brows furrowed. 'One murder every day. Here?'

'Well,' – Mouldy Moulton's gin appeared – 'sudden deaths. One chap keeled over in the middle of a speech and another set fire to his flat. Pretty funny.'

'Ach,' said Franz. 'Your English sense of humour.'

'Funny peculiar,' said Moulton. 'Not funny ha-ha.'

Poor Doktor Gottlieb frowned even harder. Moulton

grinned and pulled a small pouch from his pocket out of which he took something that looked very like an eye dropper. He squeezed it over his glass and a dribble of angostura bitters hit the gin.

'Barman's friend,' he said. 'Present from Freddie Grimaldi.'

Bognor experienced a lurching thrill of forensic intuition.

'What is it, exactly?' he asked, faux-naif.

'Exactly that,' said Mouldy. 'Nobody in the world seems capable of mixing a pink gin the way I like it. In, not out, and not less than three drops of pink, not more than four. With this little hooshmy-bangmy I can control my input precisely.'

'So you take it with you everywhere?'

'Absolutely. Don't leave home without it.'

How often, thought Bognor, did advertising slogans become the everyday currency of cocktail party chatter? Not only that they passed for wit. In this instance American Express had a lot to answer for.

'Was Freddie in the habit of dishing these things out?'

Moulton appeared to think for a moment.

'I suppose we were in the same line of business, so it was a natural prezzie from one booze-wallah to another. I know Seymour Puce has one because I've had one of his Scarpington Specials. He couldn't do it like Freddie, alas. That particular secret died with him.'

Bognor felt his brain clanking. It was as if the night shift of midgets that lurked in his cranium had been suddenly bundled out of bed to deal with a red alert. He had a vision of battalions of bleary-eyed termites shovelling the grey matter from one side of his head to the other while the two competing majors i/c brain cells barked contradictory instructions at their insubordinates.

'Suppose Mouldy Moulton wanted to kill Reg Brackett.'

'Why suppose?'

'Let us suppose ... he could have dosed his port with a lethal dose from his barman's friend.'

'A lethal dose of what?'

'A lethal dose of a poisonous substance ...'

'Unknown to medical science, tasteless, odourless, quick-acting and undetectable by pathologist at post-mortem. Pull the other one, major.'

'With respect, major, life is full of surprises but ne'er so full as death.'

The brain activity was frenetic, tumultuous, unlikely to produce a solution for a while. Bognor tried to relegate it to his subconscious. Out loud he said to Moulton, 'How interesting. May I see?'

Moulton obliged.

It was *very* like a nose or eye dropper. A bulbous rubber sachet at one end, then a glass tube about two and a half inches long. A gentle squeeze would discharge a single droplet of whatever the bulb contained. It was small enough to conceal in the palm of a hand, easy to use. A practised performer could have introduced any liquid he liked into almost anything whatever without being observed. Neat. Almost the perfect murder weapon.

'What a good idea,' he said, and then again because the clamouring in his brain was distracting him, he repeated the phrase, 'what a good idea'.

The message from the brain was beginning to assume a modicum of coherence. What it said, roughly, up to a point and in a manner of speaking, was that if Reg Brackett had been murdered then it could have been done by a man – or woman – armed with a 'barman's friend' who introduced a substance – as yet unknown – into his drink. It now emerged that Freddie himself possessed one of these said 'barman's friends'; likewise Sir Seymour Puce; and Augustus 'Mouldy' Moulton. Any one of the three could therefore, in theory, have committed the murder. Always provided they could have got close enough to Reg's glass. But then, if Grimaldi the barman was in the habit of dishing out 'barman's friends' to all and sundry the field of suspects was so enlarged as to become unmanageable.

He was saved by Sir Seymour who reminded him of the old saw about the back-bench MP who dreamt that he was making a speech in the House of Commons and then woke up to find that he was. When two or more were gathered together in his presence Sir Seymour would make a speech at them. 'If it moves,' ran the military maxim, 'salute it.' There were other versions, some harmless such as 'paint it', some too sexual to bear repetition. In Sir Seymour's case the reaction to other members of the human race was to clear his throat, raise his hand to his lapel, and harangue them. As far as he was concerned the only collective noun for 'people' was 'audience'.

Thus tonight at the Bog Sir Seymour's response was Pavlovian and inevitable. It began, 'Meine Damen und Herren, Ladies and Gentlemen, On behalf of Scarpington Thursday Football Club, Good Evening, Welcome, Thank you for joining us on such an auspicious occasion, and may you all have a very enjoyable and memorable evening, here together, tonight.'

Bognor switched off at this point and fell to contemplating the company. Apart from Nigel Festing and Edna Fothergill, who, he supposed, were hard at it on the black waterbed in The Laurels (unless put off their stroke by the unexpected intervention of himself and the Countess) it looked like a near-total turnout of Artisan brass mixing with the Frankfurters. The only additions were one or two younger members of both sexes who might conceivably have been cadet Artisans, children of the middle-aged burghers, the next generation of the no longer silent majority. Several of them had the deep tan that Britain cannot offer without benefit of sunbed. The men looked as if they already drove BMWs and were 'learning the business' by shunting from one department of daddy's firm to another in a 'pretend' menial capacity. The women veered towards pulchritude, expensive bangles and the first hints of a dangerous boredom. Well, thought Bognor, the Bridge Club should soon take care of that.

Depressed by the company and the orotund drone of Puce's welcome, his gaze was drawn to the terraces filling up below. The inflatable éclairs were quite impressive now and some enterprising huckster had produced some rubber hot-dogs to represent the German team.

Suddenly a face in the crowd caught his attention. Unlike the others, it was turned up to the stand where the directors and their guests were gathered. It was on top of a Burberry-style trench coat of the type favoured by the police in black and white B movies – heavily buckled and belted. Clearly something about the directors' box was fascinating the face but it was too far away to be able to recognise anyone with absolute certainty. Besides it was dark and although the directors' area was well illuminated the stand areas were murky by comparison. Even so Bognor was fairly sure that he was right and that he had correctly identified the figure in the mac.

Wartnaby.

If so, the Detective Chief Inspector was taking a risk. He was supposed to be lying low, although on the other hand just because he had been taken off the Brackett case was no reason, surely, for not being allowed out to a football match. Odd, though. Wartnaby had not struck Bognor as your average Scarpington Thursday fan. Perhaps after all he was mistaken – bad light, distance, a surfeit of Parsnip. He doubted whether a jury would accept his sighting. He stared out at the crowd, straining for a second glimpse, but he was unable to locate the figure a second time.

Blinking, he turned back for Puce's peroration and a formal, lukewarm round of applause. Down below them the teams were running out onto the pitch – Lokomotiv in black and white stripes, Scarpington in their unique fuchsia and gold quartered shirts. The glass slid aside and the official party made their way to the directors' box in the stand. Bognor found himself sitting between Moulton and Dr Gottlieb, the brewer, in the row immediately behind Puce and the most senior of the top brass. It was miserably chill but everyone was thoughtfully provided with vivid tartan rugs, made in Hong Kong by Puce Knitwear Plc. Moulton, thoughtfully, had not only brought his barman's friend but also an ample hip flask of home-made sloe gin. Almost without thinking Bognor allowed himself a sip and settled down to be bored.

In this he was not disappointed. Billed as a 'friendly', the game seemed to Bognor to be ill-tempered, petulant and characterised by what was universally accepted as the 'professional foul' but which he had always been brought up to regard as cheating. The Scarpington players seemed to be initially at fault but the Germans soon started to retaliate, though unlike the home team they displayed flashes of skill and what Bognor knew the football correspondents sometimes described as 'artistry'.

'Very physical team, Thursday,' said Moulton, passing the flask.

'Physical,' repeated Bognor.

'The continentals play a much less physical game.'

'Ah,' said Bognor.

'Pretty-pretty. All very well to watch but it doesn't get results.' Moulton chewed on a slurp of sloe gin. 'See what I mean?' he asked, nodding towards the pitch. One of the Lokomotiv players had nutmegged his marker with considerable dexterity only to be scythed down by a Thursday defender who seemed to jump into the small of his back from behind.

'Is that legal?' asked Bognor.

'Ref might blow up in a league match,' said Moulton, 'but as this is a friendly he lets it go.'

Could this be a metaphor for life? Bognor was unclear. His own observations over a middle-aged lifetime led him to believe that, among the English, all was fair in love but not in war, that they, that is we, took pleasures seriously but business frivolously. In football, it appeared, one was allowed to cheat in a friendly match but not in an unfriendly one. This was Thatcherite *laissez-faire* gone mad. Oh God, he should never have drunk so much. Oh God, he missed his wife. Oh God, he wished he was in bed.

In front of him Sir Seymour was video-ing the game with a neat Videopuce Camcorder manufactured in the Philippines. He was doing it with all the ostentatious effortlessness of the passionate and competitive amateur.

At the same time he was lecturing the chief kraut, some

sort of burgomeister figure, sitting on his right. 'Now,' Bognor heard, 'you've selected your high speed shutter, so your depth of field is going to be reduced, especially at the higher speeds. OK. So you open the aperture right up to get the correct exposure. And for the same reason your focus has to be more accurate because when the objects get close the focal lengths get longer.'

His German guest nodded vigorously and said 'Ja, Ja.' Boring Puce might be, but he was obviously an authentic video freak. Bognor might not know a SCART connector from a 51cm FST tube, but he could always tell an expert in his own subject. Sir Seymour was talking shop, but he was talking the shop of the shopkeeper.

'Now,' he said, 'suppose I want to edit from a GR-C1 camcorder to an HR-D530 mains deck. Simple ...' But just as he was about to explain there was a groan from the crowd as the Lokomotiv striker was scythed down from behind by the Thursday left back. There was a shrill blast of the whistle and the referee pointed to the penalty spot.

'Bloody ref,' said Mouldy Moulton. 'Doesn't he know it's just a friendly?'

Sir Seymour was on his feet, still filming but also shouting at the referee to reconsider. Inflatable éclairs and hot dogs jostled each other on the terracing. A chorus of 'off, off, off' mingled with another of 'ref, ref, ref'. The ref showed the erring Thursday man a yellow card, the Lokomotiv striker placed the ball on the spot and struck it casually past the home goalkeeper to a chorus of whistles and polite applause from the German bigwigs in the directors' box. In his excitement Puce had knocked over a box of tapes on the table-top immediately in front of his chair. Straining hard, Bognor tried to work out what the handwritten title said. When he did manage to read it he let out a little sigh which signified realisation and a sudden recognition that perhaps a trap was beginning to close. The handwritten legend on the side of the video-tape said: 'Bridge, The Laurels, Nov 17th'.

'Aha,' said Bognor to himself. 'Seymour Puce, the Russ Meyer of Wedgwood Benn Gardens.'

CHAPTER EIGHT

'If you don't go to other men's funerals, they won't go to yours'

Wartnaby was dead on time. Full fry-up, another *cafetière* of his exotic coffee from Kilimanjaro, and the papers which carried the news of last night's unsatisfactory defeat under such headings as 'Thursday run out of puff v Locos', 'Scarpington come off the rails' and 'End of the line at the Bog'.

'Bring porridge, bring sausage, bring fish for a start,' sang Wartnaby in a bath-baritone.

> Bring kidneys and mushrooms and partridges' legs,
> But let the foundation be bacon and eggs.

This early morning jollity left Bognor less than cold.

'Did I see you out at the Bog last night?' he asked.

'The what?'

'The Bog. The local football ground. I thought I saw you in the crowd.'

Wartnaby looked incredulous in a civilised, non-censorious way.

'Hardly my scene at the best of times,' he said, 'and frankly I'm keeping an exceedingly low profile. This is my first trip out of doors since yesterday's breakfast. I have to be exceedingly careful. I don't think you quite realise how insidiously powerful these wretched Artisans are.'

'Oh, don't bank on it.' Bognor glanced at the black pudding and eggs and bacon and mushrooms and fried bread and sausage and tomato and decided that one could not be anything other than grateful to a man who could bring all this to your room, even if he did insist on singing the while. And flat. He tucked a napkin into the top of his Viyella pyjamas and began to eat.

'So,' said Wartnaby, leaning against the wall and gazing through the double glazing at the city below. 'How was your day?'

'You sound just like my wife,' said Bognor through a mouthful of health hazard. 'But I did learn a thing or two.'

'Like what?'

'Like,' Bognor chewed thoughtfully and chose his words with rather more care than he devoted to his diet, 'Like what the Artisans are really up to.'

'You went to Moulton and Bragg?' Bognor's subconscious told him that the DCI's nonchalance was assumed, that he was not as languid and devil-may-care as he chose to seem.

'I did indeed. But I also went to The Laurels in Wedgwood Benn Gardens.'

Long pause.

'Should that mean something?' Wartnaby appeared genuinely perplexed. He seemed to be implying that Wedgwood Benn Gardens was not his neck of the woods.

'It's the Artisan Club. We discussed it yesterday.'

'I'm sorry.' Wartnaby was engrossed in his coffee. Or the view from the window. Or both. In either event he was abstracted. Not entirely of the world at this precise moment in time. Then, as if he was hearing it for the first time, he repeated, 'You went to The Laurels in Wedgwood Benn Gardens.'

'That's what I said.' Wartnaby might have provided one of the world's great breakfasts, but Bognor was not going to be patronised and taken for granted by him. Bognor had gone out on a limb for him, infiltrating The Laurels like that. He wanted more than breakfast. He wanted gratitude.

Wartnaby obviously realised.

'I'm sorry,' he said. 'I wasn't concentrating properly. That's quite a coup. How did you manage it?'

Bognor told him about the Countess and Piggy's key. Then he described everything about the club up until he'd discovered the 'Bridge' section. As soon as he mentioned this Wartnaby began to perk up.

'Is it bridge they play there?' asked Wartnaby. 'Or is that just a front? I thought that score card I found at Grimaldi's extremely suspicious. The odd numbers. The hint of the arbitrary. The inverted commas round "bridge". Did you discover the truth?'

Oh, but Bognor loved black pudding. What was truth, even ultimate truth, beside black pudding? Bother cholesterol; knickers to calories. He chewed, he swallowed, and finally he spoke.

'Sex,' he said. 'Not bridge, but sex.'

'Sex.' Wartnaby said it as if he had never heard the word before. The inflexion he gave it suggested mild distaste, but only mild. 'Sex,' he repeated. 'You mean, as in intercourse.'

'Wife-swapping,' said Bognor. 'On waterbeds.'

'Waterbeds.' Wartnaby sounded like a high court judge suddenly confronted, in very mature years, with the notion of a 'G string' or 'sting'. He drew the word out very long, like Lady Bracknell saying 'handbag'.

Bognor explained about Nigel Festing and Edna Fothergill.

'It's just the way they do it in squash clubs,' said Bognor, relying now on second-hand sources. 'Only because you can't have an out and out winner you have to have marks like figure skating or synchronised swimming. And, being the Scarpington Artisans' Bridge Club, you get marks for manners.'

'Please and thank you,' said Wartnaby.

'Just so,' said Bognor.

'And in order to award these marks,' the Inspector scowled, 'there have to be adjudicators. Unless it's like the GCSE and you do a continual assessment?'

Bognor told him about the two-way mirror and the 'viewing room'. Then he told him about Sir Seymour Puce and his video camera at the Thursday–Lokomotiv clash.

'QED,' he said, when he'd finished. 'In effect, Sir Seymour is running a do-it-yourself vice ring.' He drank some of Wartnaby's Kibo Chagga, savouring it like good claret.

'Very interesting,' said Wartnaby. 'Very interesting indeed. But we still have no proof that Puce murdered Reg Brackett and Freddie Grimaldi.'

'Is the result of Brackett's post-mortem through?' asked Bognor. 'It's his funeral this morning, I thought I'd drift along.'

'I'm sure it's through,' said Wartnaby. 'But I daren't ask. More than my job's worth. What's left of it.' He smiled ruefully. 'The trouble is that, as I've said before, Puce has this town sewn up. Knowing that he's a double murderer is one thing. Proving it is quite another.'

'Mouldy Moulton has a barman's friend,' said Bognor, and when Wartnaby confessed that he did not know what a barman's friend was he told him, adding, 'So he could easily have Micky Finned a drink of Reg's some time during the evening.'

'But why,' asked Wartnaby, 'would Moulton want to do that? He and Brackett got on perfectly well. Their businesses didn't overlap.'

'You said Brackett called on the Scarpingtons? Presumably to try and get money out of him because of the ailing laundry. So my guess,' said Bognor, 'is that he tried blackmailing Piggy Scarpington.'

'Piggy?'

'That's what the Countess calls him.'

'Of course,' said Wartnaby. 'I'd forgotten you were so close to the Countess. But how could he have blackmailed the Earl?'

'Because the Earl was into the Bridge Club.'

'So was practically everybody else in town, by the look of it.' Wartnaby stroked his chin. 'Safety in numbers. That would be the theory. That and, no doubt, some mad pseudo-masonic curse involving tongue extraction for divulging the secrets of the third apron.'

'Perhaps that's it. Perhaps it's a ritual murder.' Bognor, fortified by the fry-up, and now chomping doorsteps of toast and marmalade, sensed his intuitive and deductive powers moving into a high imaginative gear. 'Perhaps Brackett was so desperate about the finances of the laundry that he infringed Artisan law by threatening to break the secrets of the Bridge Club. So the only possible response, according to the Ancient Ritual and Lore of the Artisans, was for them to do him in. Just like the Ayatollah and Rushdie,' he said, remembering the slogan on the railway bridge in the Muslim quarter of town. 'Poor old Ayatollah had no alternative but to pass sentence on Rushdie because the penalty for blasphemy was written down in the Koran. Same with Brackett. I bet it's all there in the sacred Artisan law book, so Puce had no choice but to declare a "fatwa", and order Brackett's ritual slaughter a.s.a.p. Big reward to the Artisan who actually accomplished it.'

'If,' Wartnaby was looking doubtful, 'we accept the premise, then what about Freddie?'

'Well,' said Bognor, 'without actually having access to the ancient Artisan rule book it's difficult to be certain, but how about running this one up the flagpole? How about the Artisans appointing Freddie Grimaldi as the weapon of their wrath and then when he had done the deed he too has to die.'

'Mmmm.' Wartnaby looked at his watch. 'Isn't that a touch fanciful?'

'The whole thing is fanciful,' said Bognor. 'I came down here to write an official government-sponsored paper on trade and industry in the most boring provincial city anyone could think of. It should have been a long, tedious document about hard work and computers and thrift and respectability. I had expected something terribly terribly English in a nice, genteel, cosy tradition. "Cosy", in fact, is precisely the word I'm looking for. I thought it was all going to be wonderfully bland and cosy. Well no one can accuse the Scarpington Artisans of being cosy. It's mayhem. Sex and violence and vice and corruption in every shape or form.'

'And yet still cosy, despite everything.' Wartnaby was being philosophical. 'It's the English way,' he said, *'toujours la politesse. Foreigners can't understand it. They like their sex and violence underdone. Sanglant.* Practically raw. We, on the other hand, conceal it behind net curtains and antimacassars. On the Continent a brothel is a brothel is a brothel. Here it's a bridge club. Look at Cynthia Payne: Earl Grey and charades and middle-aged tarts in gymslips. Too too terribly polite and civilised. Even now when we're contemplating crude lust of an almost totally animal kind we still bowdlerise it by talking about "going to bed with each other" or "hanky-panky" or even, God help us, about "making love"! Nigel Festing and Edna Fothergill were no more going to make love with one another than a couple of ferrets.'

Bognor thought this unfair to ferrets even though he had to acknowledge the essential truth of what the Detective Chief Inspector was saying. Much of his life had been dedicated to proving the proposition that in Britain both sin and crime were so hedged about with convention, good manners, wearing the right clothes, having been at the correct school and above all never being common or vulgar that they became effectively unrecognisable as sin or crime. What was taking place here in the middle of England was yet another example. He sighed. 'So, as a working hypothesis, let us assume that Brackett was killed according to the corporate will of the Artisans and that Freddie, the barman, was the instrument of that will, using his special nose dropper to introduce an alien substance into Brackett's drink. Then a person unknown sets fire to Grimaldi. Who he?'

'Puce,' said Wartnaby.

'How so?' Bognor considered this second clipped interrogatory response evidence of further sharp thinking. He was feeling more on the ball than at any time since arriving. He would teach these villainous provincials to cosy up to him. No mere red-brick sex fiends and killer conspirators would get away from him.

'That's what we have to discover.' Wartnaby paced in

139

silence for a moment. 'In the normal course of events,' he said, 'I would, of course, question Puce about his whereabouts at the time in question. And, Artisans apart, I would be particularly interested in the size of his shareholding in Mr Clean and Bleach'n'Starch.'

'How big is it?'

'I'm led to believe it's "substantial",' said Wartnaby.

'In Mr Clean *and* Bleach'n'Starch?'

'Puce doesn't do things by halves.'

'It certainly doesn't look like it.' Bognor was impressed by Wartnaby's apparent mastery of the Puce dossier. Even so . . .

'Are you certain that Puce is the villain of the piece?'

'Villain of the piece' had an oddly official ring to it. Almost as suggestive of pillar of society as Justice of the Peace, which, of course, Sir Seymour already was. Sir Seymour Puce, VP, PS, JP. The backbone of England as represented by the Artisans and men like Puce was obsessed by initials after surnames just as it was by gongs to wear round the neck at formal dinners. It was part, thought Bognor, of what made Britain so spineless.

'I feel it,' said Wartnaby. 'There is the smell of corruption in him and its reek permeates the whole of this society.'

Bognor had never, to the best of his knowledge, had to deal with a crusader policeman before. He found it disturbing, but better that than the bent copper. Or so he supposed.

'I think we had better beard Puce in his den,' said Wartnaby.

'You mean, see him at Puce International or the House of Commons?' Bognor was not sure he saw the point of either.

'No, no.' Wartnaby shook his head. 'Den of iniquity. The Laurels. Confront him with his turpitude and wring a confession from him.'

'Isn't that a bit risky?' Bognor was getting fed up with risks.

'Time's not on my side,' said Wartnaby, glancing at his watch. 'And it's a case of Puce or me. If I don't take the initiative then he will. If I let him get the upper hand he'll have me out of the force altogether.'

'So what do you want me to do?'

'Inveigle him into The Laurels. Get him to confess and I'll be there to witness.' Bognor looked dubious, which he was.

'It has to be done.' Wartnaby flashed a smile. 'And done quickly. Otherwise we'll both be undone. Once Puce and the Artisans decide that you're trying to dish the dirt on them, they'll have you out of a job too. Or worse. Look what happened to Brackett and Grimaldi.'

Wartnaby picked up a Jolly Trencherman notepad from alongside the Gideons' Bible on Bognor's bedside table. 'As soon as you've made an appointment with Puce,' he said, 'ring this number. I shan't answer. Just let it ring for the number of hours you've fixed. I suggest six rings for six o'clock sharp for preference. If you don't call I'll be back here for breakfast, but I'd much prefer an interview today. The kitchens are beginning to get suspicious.'

He seemed about to disappear but paused at the door. 'Oh,' he said, 'if you have time, I think you should have a look at Ron Brown. He's succeeded Reg Brackett as President of Artisans, which is interesting in itself. He failed to be made President once before. Something to do with contaminated yoghurt, or so I'm led to believe. Also, like all the others he's crazy for an honour, even if it's only an MBE like poor little Reg. And, of course, Puce is the fount from which all such honours flow. I think a word with Ron might not come amiss. He has an office above Ye Milke and Yoghurte Bar in Dean's Byre just next door to the Cope and Cripple.'

'Right,' said Bognor. 'I'll do what I can.'

And this time Wartnaby did make his exit. It was funny, thought Bognor, about the Bog last night. Wartnaby's macintosh was just like the belted and buckled Burberry he had noticed in the crowd. But then it was quite a common style. All he could honestly swear to have seen was a man in a mac. He gazed at the breakfast tray. There was still a slice of toast and some butter left on it. He was very tempted but he knew that he had had enough. So to prove that he was made of stern stuff he took the tray and put it outside on the carpet of the corridor. The gesture cheered him up a little.

Still, he did feel lonely and neglected. Not even a phone call from Parkinson. It was a bit much. Here he stood, like a Roman centurion on Hadrian's Wall, far from home, lashed by alien elements, contemplating the hostile hordes, and there was no support from home. Even Diana, the Countess, fickle jade, had retreated to the bright lights of London. Monica, he could, in fairness, hardly blame. But one's own boss! He thought mutinously of putting in a call to Parkinson, reversing the charges, of course, but the thought of that martinet's voice gimletting into him with its sharp, unsympathetic queries, its 'Why in God's name are you wasting my time and the Board's money on your mindless whinges?' and its 'In pity's name, use the talents the Good Lord provided you with and tell us all what goes on out there' was more than he could bear. Scott must have felt like this in the Antarctic; or Hillary and Tenzing, Mallory and Irving as they battled toward the summit of Everest. This was Indian country; he was John Wayne and there was no sign of the cavalry. He experienced a sudden stab of indigestion and wondered for a terrible moment if some unknown enemy had nobbled the Kibo Chagga coffee with a dose from their barman's friend.

At times like this, adrift in a sea of doubt and deceptive tranquillity, it was his custom to make a list of suspects together with motive and opportunity, the better to concentrate his mind. He knew that this was probably what he should do and yet the effort was too much and the reasons less than compelling. All roads led to Puce and they all led via this extraordinary society, so drab and mundane and, yes, admit it, so cosy on the surface, yet so reptilian, corrupt and sinister within. How much more dangerous were these smiling, familiar breweries and factories and football grounds than the mean streets of Los Angeles and Detroit or the battlefields of Far East Asia. One knew if one consulted statistics that it was everyday life that threatened, not the exotics of foreign travel. Yet it was not until one experienced the chilling dangers of the commonplace face to face that one quite realised the truth of this self-evident fact. Risk lay in the day-to-day, not the once-in-a-lifetime. Death came changing the light bulb while standing on the bathroom floor or crossing the road to catch the last post. Here in Scarpington where everything seemed so damnably dull, this was where one learned to walk in mortal dread.

Bognor shivered.

It was ten-thirty. Brackett's funeral was at noon. If he set off now he would have time to case Ye Olde Dairy and hope to find Ron Brown at home. No point in telephoning in advance. Much better to take him unawares and hope to catch him in the act of who knows what – having his way with a buxom milkmaid, fiddling his VAT return, adulterating his products – Bognor could believe anything.

His Arkwright and Blennerhasset was loud for a funeral, especially here where they so respected convention and conformity. This was a black-tie job. He was already wearing the trousers, with braces, of an off-the-peg grey worsted two-piece, which would have passed unnoticed at a convention of bank managers. He was already wearing a white shirt so plain and unremarkable that it could have been worn to school by a new boy at King's Scarpington. His shoes were scuffed but black by origin and design, and, like royalty, he always travelled with a plain black tie, 'just in case'. This was not mere empty superstition. Too often in his life he had set off on a job which began as a jaunt only to find himself a few days later sitting dry-eyed in a funeral pew listening to the last post sound for a newly and unexpectedly deceased.

He knotted the tie four times before getting it quite right, drained the dregs of the coffee, fluffed up the white handkerchief in his jacket pocket and preened himself in the mirror. What could be more funereal? Give him an opera hat and he could have done service as a professional mute. 'It is better,' he told himself, 'to go to the house of mourning,

143

than to go to the house of feasting: for that is the end of all men; and the living will lay it to his heart.' That was one of the things about an expensive old-fashioned education. You had an apt 'mot' for every moment – though if you believed that particular piece of Old Testament claptrap you'd believe anything. 'Ho hum,' he said to himself and left the room whistling. Funerals often made him feel cheery.

It was not, he thought, market day and yet he was acutely aware of people shopping. He personally detested shopping and Monica was not keen either. The Bognors shopped to live but Simon had a keen impression that Scarpingtonians this morning were living to shop. He had originally thought that his route to Dean's Byre was unimpeded, but when it came to actually walking the ground and not just looking at a map, he discovered that his way was blocked by a vast concrete edifice called 'The Sludgelode Centre' *sic*. This was part multi-storey car park, part multi-storey shopping arcade, and it was absolutely jam-packed with shoppers.

Yet these shoppers were not, on the evidence of what Bognor could see for himself, shopping for the staff of life. They were shopping for complete Scarpington Thursday football kits; electric pencil sharpeners; magazines with titles like *The Complete Countrywoman*, *Royal Hats*, *Practical Rollerskating* and *Tablecloth*; orange parakeets; designer jeans; pink tracksuit trousers; Slimeazee Paella Valenciana with brown rice; filofaxes; fairly naughty black knickers and suspender belts with red hearts on them; lopsided mugs which said 'Holidays make me tipsy'; conventional mugs which said 'I "heart" Scarpington'; cut-price excursions to Thailand; confetti; PVC aprons covered with advertisements for long-forgotten vinegar-based sauces; brushes for brushing mushrooms; machines for taking the pips out of papayas; individual cocktail-shaker-shaped helpings of Planter's Punch; postcards of Marilyn Monroe; posters of James Dean; the 'Complete Jeffrey Archer'; games of Trivial Pursuit.

The only bread was 'organically grown wholewheat nutgerm from SelfEmploy Farms of Wendover-on-the-Sludgelode'; the only wine was Peruvian Cabernet or Dandelion and Burdock from the same SelfEmploy Farmers that made the bread (and who appeared to be 'By Appointment to His Royal Highness the Prince of Wales'); the only milk seemed to come from goats.

Perhaps Bognor was mistaken. Perhaps he only saw what he wanted to see. Perhaps his experiences of Scarpington so far had made him unnaturally jaundiced so that he saw this great demonstration of British affluence through bilious pale yellow spectacles. And wasn't it, in any case, so much better than the bad old days of the antimacassar factory when the men wore clogs and the only show in town was Scarpington Thursday and ''ee son, you queued for a loaf of bread in them days' and ate it, of course, with a scrape of dripping and no one in the town outside the Castle and the Bishop's Palace had ever clapped eyes on a fresh grapefruit. Let alone teeth.

And it was rather wonderful that you could have real waterfalls and fountains, indoors, in the very middle of Scarpington. And it was exciting to be able to look up and see a whole flock of Scarpington geese specially sculpted by a world-famous local sculptor suspended from the magnificent domed glass roof. And when you thought what life had been like only a decade or so ago when the nation had practically ground to a halt and the unions were too big for their boots (or clogs) and the teachers were on strike and the dead lay around unburied because there was no one to work the crematoria, and Britain was 'the sick man of Europe', well, it made you think, didn't it?

Bognor thought of the Artisans and the Bridge Club and Mouldy Moulton and Nigel Festing and Edna Fothergill and above all Sir Seymour Puce; and a nasty, pseudo-puritanical, self-righteous streak of moral indignation briefly asserted itself. For one reprehensible second he had an attack of the retired majors and found himself saying that maybe it wouldn't be such a bad idea to bring back national service and the rope and the birch and the cat and ration books and National Health orange juice and, yes, maybe even clogs. And then he shook himself and reminded himself that he had never known poverty, and he had no right, no right at all, and he turned up his coat and hurried on through to the other side.

Ye Olde Dairy or Ye Olde Milke and Yoghurte Bar was, as he had suspected, a chip off the Sludgelode Centre block. It could equally well have been called 'Ye Olde Ice Cream Parlour'. It was a riot of chrome and cream, mirrors and high bar stools, and potted ferns. There was a juke box and young men and women in black and white paying their way through Technical College. Bognor was reminded of an Edward Hopper painting, of an image of small-town or suburban America brought across the Atlantic, de-sleazed and given a contemporary Scarpington chic. A year or so ago it might have been as coronary-inducing as Bognor's hotel breakfast, but in deference to another turn of the fashion dial this was, with a very few exceptions, determinedly healthy and designer lean. Thus 'Kiwi Shake made with skim milk and low fat yoghurt', 'Carrot and Mango Sundae', 'Walnut, Carob and Quark Gateau'. In vain did Bognor look for Knickerbocker Glory or Banana Split or Hot Fudge Sundae, though one or two items did have an asterisk by them which turned out to indicate that this particular concoction was made with 'full fat natural dairy ice cream'. These were not advised for those customers suffering from 'obesity, high blood pressure or who are in any way allergic to conventional dairy produce.' The note concluded, 'If in doubt, consult a doctor'.

Bognor asked a spotty youth with a shaven head and an earring if Mr Ronald Brown was in. The youth said he would see and who should he say it was. Bognor flashed his ID and thought of breakfast which was not a good idea. He didn't suppose for a second that Brown had killed either Brackett or Grimaldi, but part of a detective's job was to eliminate suspects and if he could help the grounded Wartnaby to eliminate the odd Artisan then that was a good thing. Besides which, Brown and his dairy were definitely high on his Board of Trade shopping list. He knew he could expect a serious grilling from Parkinson and Co. on the subject of 'Trends in the British Dairy Industry: Whither Milk?'

The youth returned.

Mr Brown was in a meeting but would not be more than five minutes. If Mr Bognor would like to accept an ice cream or a drink with Mr Brown's compliments he would be only too happy to assist when his meeting was concluded. Bognor said that he would be happy to wait but not to accept the boss's hospitality. He never ate between meals. This was a lie but it seemed a polite excuse.

After ten minutes of sitting on an uncomfortable stool contemplating the depressing menu with its depressing ersatz-enthusiastic way with the English language Bognor was told by the youth that Mr Brown would see him now.

He was ushered through a mirrored door into an altogether less glitzy atmosphere where there was lino on the floor and no sound but the gentle click of fingers on computer keyboards and the hum and whirr of printers printing. Hi-tech dairy business – a computerised creamery.

'Mr Bognor, welcome to the Cream of the Country's Dairies.' Ronald Brown, husband, Bognor could not help thinking, of Dorothy Brown who had scored three in the bridge evening whose card Wartnaby had shown him, rose and shook Bognor's hand. Three points was only one more, thought Bognor, than poor old Mouldy Moulton and a good six less than Harold Fothergill. He wondered what division Ronald was in.

'Would you care for a Fruitybrown?' asked Ronald.

'A Fruitybrown?' said Bognor.

'Nutmeg, cinnamon, molasses, fig or nut,' said Ronald. 'All preservative-free set yoghurts with real fruit, nuts, spices or what have you. Cartonned in our brand new plant at Sludgelode Fen. Fruitybrown is the brand leader in the UK short-shelf-life, high-health dairy products market north of the Trent.'

'I see,' said Bognor. This was grist to Parkinson's mill, though not perhaps to Wartnaby's. 'Which do you recommend?'

Mr Brown regarded him carefully. 'You look a bit peaky, if I might say so. If I were you I'd have a Fig Fruitybrown. That'll set you up.'

The dairyman pressed a button on a box on his desk and said into it, 'Maeve. Could you let us have a couple of Fig Fruitybrowns in my office.' He spoke, Bognor noticed, with an air of confident, if limited, authority. Like Bognor he was funereally dressed, all in black, save for the white shirt front. Even his face, which was slablike and flabby, had a pallor which might have been donned specially for Reg Brackett's obsequies. He was, Bognor supposed, just the wrong side of fifty. Unremarkable, but a pillar of the community. And of the Artisan Bridge Club.

'Saw you at the game last night,' said Ron. 'Sorry I didn't have an opportunity to communicate. I was having to entertain two of their big cheese makers. Sir Seymour has persuaded me to take a consignment, though I'm not at all sure it'll catch on. It's very high fat and full of caraway seed. Still they are taking a tanker of Fruitybrown in part exchange.' He sighed. 'Very poor game. I've been watching Thursday, man and boy, for almost half a century. They don't make them like they used to. You going to poor Reg Brackett's funeral?'

Bognor said he was. Ron had presumably realised that Bognor was not normally given to wearing a black tie.

'Poor Reginald.' Ron looked genuinely distressed. 'Known him all my life. Very nice man. Very decent, God-fearing, did a tremendous amount for local charities. I remember him dressing up as Father Christmas year after year for the annual Artisan children's party. He was a surprisingly good Father Christmas for such a shy man. I think sheltering behind the beard did it. A sort of disguise. Gave him confidence. Perhaps if he'd been able to dress up as Father Christmas all the time he'd have enjoyed being President of the Artisans more.'

'He didn't like it?' Bognor was surprised. 'I thought it was the acme of Artisan ambition.'

The dairy owner looked at him with suspicion. 'Too shy,'

148

he said. 'Every time he had to make a speech in public he had to go and sit in the loo and compose himself. Couldn't eat his dinner. He didn't touch his food the other night before he . . . passed away. Just pushed it round his plate. Muriel didn't want him to take the presidency on. He'd had heart trouble. In fact there was talk of a by-pass, but they left it too late.'

'Do we know it was a heart attack?'

Bognor asked it mildly enough, but Ron seemed most disconcerted, though saved by the entrance of Maeve with two cartons of Fig Fruitybrown and a couple of teaspoons.

Ron's body language said 'pas devant les enfants'. Or the staff. So they were silent until Maeve left again; both making a performance of removing the foil lid, plunging the spoon into the creamy brown sludge, and tasting. Bognor identified fig and yoghurt. The overall effect was medicinal but not inedible. There was something encouraging and unusual in eating food which felt as if it was doing you good, and the Fruitybrown had the unexpected effect of buoying him up.

'Mmmmm!' he said.

'You like it?' enquired Ron.

'Very interesting.'

'I'll send a crate round to your hotel. You are staying at the Talbot, aren't you?'

Bognor hadn't reckoned on this, but what could he say? Perhaps he could pass some on to Wartnaby at breakfast.

'You were saying . . .' said Ron as the door closed behind Maeve.

'About poor Reg.'

'The heart attack. Well, yes, I mean I can only assume. Dr Dick said as much and we all knew the history so one can only conclude.'

'But there would have been a post-mortem?'

Ron waved this aside.

'Of course. Things have to be done properly, but it's just a formality. I don't think there's any doubt in anyone's mind.'

The doubt in Bognor's mind was, of course, that the one person who benefited from Brackett's death was Ron Brown, the new President of the Artisans – Lyndon Johnson to Brackett's Jack Kennedy. Or was that stretching a point? He wondered if Ron would be wearing his presidential chain of office to the funeral. Difficult point. It could be thought tasteless. But not to wear it might be considered lack of respect. To ask him would almost certainly be considered a hostile question. Bognor decided to go softly to catch this particular monkey.

'I need to know about milk,' said Bognor.

Ron brightened.

'You couldn't have come to a better place,' he said. 'I'll start at the beginning.'

And he did. After fifteen minutes they were still on milking equipment. Bognor's brain was whirring with facts and figures about the suspended bucket system and herring-bone rotary parlours and automatic cluster removals and digital flow meters for automatic milk yield recording and cow identification technology. Then they were on to cows themselves. The Common Market. Foreign competition. Did Bognor know that the French had six million cows, one million goats and 800,000 ewes and that this enormous herd produced sixty-eight million litres of milk a day?

Bognor did not. But his pencil raced across the page of his notebook. He would knock Parkinson cold with statistics like these just as he was being sandbagged himself. There was no question Ron knew his stuff.

'The French are very dangerous and unscrupulous competitors,' he continued, 'but luckily for us they've come unstuck with this listeria scare. We've now got the public alerted to the idea that the French are exporting killer cheese. And as eighty per cent of all their milk is processed into cheese and similar products we think we have them on the run. Particularly as we ourselves are well ahead of the game with pioneering products like our Fig Fruitybrown here. We're the brand leaders in this part of the world with our new additive-free cottage cheese stabilised with wholly natural milk proteins. And we've even started to take on the Frogs at their own game by building a brand new plant at Sir Seymour's industrial estate beyond the Bog where we're manufacturing a revolutionary French-style yoghurt. I'll make sure you get sent some of the prototype packs. We're calling it "Le Brun". Clever, eh? "The flavour of France from the Garden of England". We're getting that bloke from "'ello 'ello!" to do the telly commercials. He comes on with this bird in a tutu and black lace stockings and they're both eating a Le Brun yoghurt and he says, "A little bit of what you fancy does you good! Ho Ho Ho!" And she winks. I think they're going for that Linda Lusardi to play the girl. These advertising chaps think of everything.'

He paused for breath and Bognor scribbled frantically. This was, in truth, what he had come to Scarpington for.

Eventually they were through. It seemed to Bognor that there could be nothing about dairies in general and Brown's in particular that he did not know. Many might have found this boring, but not Bognor who prided himself on his open and enquiring mind. Like John Buchan he had always believed that the talk of an expert on his own subject was the best kind of conversation. Others dismissed it as shop, but not Buchan, nor Bognor.

Ron looked at his watch, a fob handed on, Bognor guessed, through generations of Browns, like the dairy itself.

'Crikey,' he said. 'We'd better go, or we'll be late for the service. And I'm reading a lesson.'

Striding through the crowded streets, Bognor said, shooting in the dark, sensing that there might be a target in the black though by no means certain what it was, 'Reg had an MBE.'

'For Community Services,' said Ron. 'They come with the rations. Not that Reginald didn't deserve it. He deserved it more than most. But even he would have been made to pay like the rest of us.'

Bognor digested this for a moment. They were walking fast and he was slightly breathless. Thought was therefore easier than speech.

'You mean Reg would have had to pay for his MBE?'

'There's another way.' The corners of Ron's fishy mouth twisted into a sardonic smile. 'You obviously haven't been in Scarpington very long.'

'No,' said Bognor. 'Only a few days.'

'Well, Mr Bognor, in Scarpington honours are paid for according to a clearly defined scale. Cash or kind both acceptable. Reg began paying cash and then ran out of money, so he switched to shares. Or so he told me. "Kind" can be any kind of kind. Personal favours, shares, invitations to one's Jamaican villa. Whatever. My deal has been strictly cash. It should come through in two years. New Year's Honours.'

'Hang on,' said Bognor, who had for some years been harbouring a modest ambition in the Honours department. In Whitehall the Order of the British Empire was the inevitable consequence of long service, however undistinguished, and Parkinson had, on occasion, let it be known or at least inferred that if Bognor kept his nose clean, didn't blot his copy book etcetera etcetera, his quarter-century at the Board of Trade – now fast approaching – might be rewarded by a modest pink ribbon with gong attached. But Honours could not be bought. Surely not? Only a lifetime of mediocrity could qualify one.

'"Contributions to party funds" is the polite way of putting it,' said Brown, 'though we all know it goes straight into the personal pocket.'

'So,' asked Bognor, 'what's the going price for an MBE?'

They were nearing the 'cathedral' now. It was, as Monica had suggested, no more than a glorified parish church, ecclesiastical acceptance of the Industrial Revolution with its concomitant population explosion. Not specially impressive, but a House of God nonetheless. It seemed sacrilegious to be discussing Mammon quite so cynically when you were almost at its portals. The tipsy, faded gravestones set in the grass outside seemed united in a stiff rebuke.

'Twenty thou, I think, and that's a single one-off payment. If you spread it then it's like any Hire-Purchase Agreement.

Financially, that is. The crucial difference is that you don't take delivery until you've made the final deposit. It's not like buying a fridge.'

'But,' Bognor paused, 'I'm not sure I understand properly. I mean, I know a bit about how the system works. I know that honours no longer flow directly from the monarch except in a few very special cases – the Royal Victorian Order and that kind of thing. But it's . . . I mean there's a system . . . and committees. It's all regulated. You can't just buy them.'

He might just have been the head of a provincial dairy, but Mr Brown now allowed himself the luxury of appearing thoroughly superior. It was agreeable, after all, to be able to patronise, all in one go, a Londoner, an Oxford graduate and a government inspector. Artisans seldom got opportunities like that, even after ten years of Thatcher.

'Surely, Mr Bognor,' he said, standing almost under the drip of a carbuncular gargoyle which leered out from the guttering by the cathedral's flying buttresses, 'you weren't born yesterday. Here in Scarpington every man has his price. Down south you may indulge in empty lies and hypocrisy, but up here we know that if you want something you damn well have to pay for it. And if you want letters after your name then you pay for that too.'

'Just for a handful of silver he left us,' said Bognor, shocked not for the first time by the revelations of provincial life. 'Just for a riband to stick in his coat.'

'My view,' said Ron, 'is that if I want a riband to stick in my coat and I've got the money to pay for it then pay for it I will. We have a saying of our own in this part of the world and maybe you've heard of it down south. Where there's muck there's brass. Where there's muck there's brass.'

And dead on cue there was a gentle purring of expensive motor as a new Rolls-Royce with the numberplate PUC 1 came to a halt just alongside.

The uniformed chauffeur alighted, raised and extended a St Moritz Toboggan Club golfing umbrella and opened the passenger door. Out stepped Sir Seymour Puce MP (Cons.) for Scarpington, a vision of power and prosperity in tailored overcoat and hand-stitched funeral gear. He even carried a silk top hat. The aura of Corona Corona and Penhaligon's after-shave shimmered about him like ectoplasm or dry ice.

'Or vice versa. Where there's brass there's muck.' Bognor turned, but Brown of Brown's Dairy had disappeared into the church to take his place in the Artisans' pew. Bognor shrugged. Looking back he watched the broad back of Sir Seymour follow in self-conscious splendour. Truly a man of brass. Bognor shivered. The original, Talus, a creation of Vulcan, used to make himself red-hot and then hug his enemies to death. Sir Seymour, guessed Bognor, would be quite capable of emulating the feat. He must be careful not to get too close.

CHAPTER NINE

'A man ought to be able to be fond of his wife without making a fool of himself about her'

Monica had been right about the banners. They were vile, garish papal yellow rags stitched by the Scarpington Townswomen's Guild by order, obviously, of some unspeakable trendy Dean. Bognor made a mental note to write to Gavin Stamp, the architectural journalist and scourge of the progressive clergy. He would enjoy reading Stamp's splenetic verdict on Scarpington, the Sludgelode Centre, the Bog, the Talbot and the Townswomen's Guild's banners in the cathedral. In among them, cobwebbed with age, were several hundred years of the regimental colours of the Fenlandshire Fusiliers. The First Battalion (the Countess of Scarpington's Own) had more battle honours than any other unit in the whole of the British Army. Their nickname was 'The Maids of Honour' and their regimental motto 'Till d'eath do us part'. They had begun life as the private army of the d'eath-Stranglefields, spreading dismay and distaste wherever they went. There was a terrible poetic and historic justice in their being upstaged by the banners of the Townswomen's Guild.

Bognor slid into a pew at the back of the church, immediately under the memorial citation to an eighteenth-century divine of otherwise total obscurity but evidently near-miraculous powers of learning, beauty of countenance, breadth of charity and all-round lightness of being.

He only just had time for a speedy agnostic prayer (just in case there was a God and just in case he had noticed) before the organ ceased and a wattling voice – the Bishop's, he guessed – intoned, 'I am the resurrection and the life, saith the Lord; he that believeth in me, though he were dead, yet shall he live; and whosoever liveth and believeth in me shall never die.'

Oh good, he thought. At least Brackett was going to be buried according to the old rites. The lurid banners were false harbingers.

The grey outdoors made it grey within and there was not enough daylight to more than faintly illuminate the Victorian stained glass. Only a few wall lights broke the crepuscular gloom of the cathedral as Reg Brackett's coffin began its long, slow progress down the nave. Bognor had half hoped for Artisan pallbearers, but these looked like professionals. The Artisans were gathered up front in pews of honour, Puce and the Earl, inevitably to the fore, with Ron Brown also unusually elevated and the other Artisans gathered round.

It was a good turn-out. Not full, but crowded. Enough to justify the phrase in Harold Fothergill's report tomorrow that 'Others present in the large congregation included . . .'. Up towards the front Bognor caught a glimpse of police uniform. Senior stuff. A lot of scrambled egg, swagger stick, leather gloves. He wondered if it could be the corrupt Chief Constable, yet another of the Scarpingtonians in Puce's pocket, the man responsible for taking Wartnaby off the case. The back of the man's head gave nothing away.

'We brought nothing into this world, and it is certain we can carry nothing out. The Lord gave and the Lord hath taken away, blessed be the Name of the Lord.'

Was it as simple as that? Bognor asked himself. Had the Lord stretched out a strong right hand and stopped Reg Brackett's ticker? Wasn't Reg Brackett a bit beneath the attention of Almighty God? Wasn't Almighty God busy with more important matters? Wasn't it more likely that a jealous dairy owner lusting after Brackett's post as president had fixed his drink while he was in the loo? Or a power-crazed MP anxious to get his hand on the laundry? Or the brewer of Old Parsnip, who, after all, had a barman's friend with which to do the deed? Or Piggy, the Earl, beating off a blackmailer? Or the dead barman, acting as the agent of the Artisans United? Or a member of the Bridge Section who lusted too much after the deceased's wife Muriel?

There was a rustle of hymn book pages. Reg Brackett was now lying in his plain oak box just below the altar and the congregation were looking for Hymn 584. Bognor too looked and found and then the organ swelled and the sons and daughters of Scarpington flung back their heads and bellowed out the words of the hymn the Artisans had made their own:

> Sons of Labour, dear to Jesus
> To your homes and work again
> Go with brave hearts back to duty
> Face the peril, bear the pain.

Bognor sang along with the rest. He was good at singing along even when he didn't agree, which he didn't. Keep your head below the parapet, sit at the back, never volunteer. It wasn't his fault he was always getting into scrapes, it really wasn't. Had there been a time when the Artisans really were the sons of Labour? Maybe, but long ago. The early Browns and Bracketts and Puces and Moultons might have been horny-handed clog wearers, but they had long since risen to positions in which the most appropriate response to poverty was to grind its face.

> Sons of Labour, think of Jesus
> As you rest your homes within
> Think of that sweet babe of Mary . . .

Steady on, this was pushing hypocrisy to dangerous limits even by the standards he had come to recognise as peculiar to the Artisans.

> Sons of Labour, pray to Jesus
> Oh, how Jesus pray'd for you.

Not to much avail. This lot were beyond prayer, beyond redemption. Bognor gazed towards the ranks of dark suit and veiled hats and old fox furs and sighed. Not a pretty sight.

> Sons of Labour, be like Jesus
> Undefiled chaste and pure
> And though Satan tempt you sorely
> By his grace you shall endure.

Bognor gulped hard, but the rest of them went on singing as if they believed every word, as if they really did hanker after chastity and purity and not other people's husbands and wives on waterbeds in Wedgwood Benn Gardens. To hear them singing you would think they did want to put Satan behind them and not pay him thousands of pounds for an MBE in the New Year's Honours list.

> Till this night of sin and sorrow
> Be for ever overpast:
> And we see the golden morrow
> Home with Jesus, home at last!

Then there was a stentorian 'Amen' and to Bognor's huge relief the hymn was over, hymn books were snapped shut and everyone took to their knees. As Bognor himself creaked down on to his hassock with an ominous snapping of joints he was aware of someone sliding into the pew beside him. He did not need to look up, for the aroma of flowery English eau-de-Cologne, of a sort of Hunter Dunnish hockey team perspiration (not in the least unpleasant), of pot-pourri and gardens and first-class railway carriages and old leather, was unmistakable. He would know his wife anywhere, blindfold and without benefit of touch.

'Monica!' he hissed.

'Shut up,' she said. 'For God's sake, have a bit of respect. You're in a bloody funeral, you appalling person.'

He bit his lip, feeling an enormous surge of relief. She was back, just as Wartnaby had predicted.

Several times in the subsequent course of the service he attempted to engage her in conversation. Once during One Corinthians Fifteen ('Why stand we in jeopardy every hour'); once when the priest said that man that is born of woman hath but a short time to live and is full of misery; and a third time in the final hymn when they were all singing:

> God be with you till we meet again;
> By His counsels guide, uphold you,
> With his sheep securely fold you;
> God be with you till we meet again.

Every time she shushed him up. Then, after Brackett had passed back down the nave followed by a weeping Muriel and a bevy of lachrymose female Bracketts and stiff-lipped male Bracketts he suddenly realised that duty called and that before he could kiss and make up with his adored wife he absolutely had to grab hold of Sir Seymour Puce and make an appointment if it were humanly possible.

He got to him just as he was about to re-enter PUC 1.

'Oh, I say, Sir Seymour, I am most extraordinarily sorry to bother you at a time like this. Simon Bognor, Board of Trade, I did enormously enjoy last night and it was extremely good of you to ask me, but I wonder if we might pursue our discussions for just a moment longer. There are one or two things about which I'm not entirely clear and if I'm to get Scarpington and its business community absolutely right then I do feel it would be of the most enormous benefit if we could fit in another little chat. Not more than a quarter of an hour or so, though if it were possible to make it later today, perhaps immediately after working hours, I mean, I wonder if, say six o'clock would be convenient and I wonder, since I've heard so much about it and it does seem to be so much an integral part of the business community here, if perhaps, well, not to mince words, I wonder if it would be possible if we were to meet up at The Laurels on Wedgwood Benn Gardens so that, perhaps we could well, well . . . er . . . well.'

Sir Seymour Puce stared down at him, for he was several inches taller than Bognor. It was the stare with which he quelled constituents who wanted him to do something about their drains or Labour MPs who tried to raise questions of gay or lesbian rights or equal opportunities. It was the way he looked at his employees whenever they were being difficult – which is to say whenever they said anything other than yes sir, please sir, three bags full. It conveyed menace, disdain coupled with an opaque, blank, flat lack of reaction which was far more alarming than anything as overt as a spoken threat or imprecation. Bognor had a sense of an eternal emptiness behind those pink, rheumy, porcine eyes. It was like contemplating an extra-terrestrial: the Kraken or *Haploteuthis ferox*.

But Bognor did not quail.

And after a silence broken only by the tolling of the cathedral bell for poor dead Reg, Sir Seymour said, 'All right. Six o'clock. The Laurels.'

Bognor watched the Roller ease away from the church, then turned back to his wife who was standing in the shelter of the Cathedral porch. He must, he told himself, try not to look smug. That would spoil everything. It was extremely satisfactory when one's mate came scuttling back to the nest so speedily and with such docility, and one was naturally pleased. But one must not show it. Women did not like that sort of thing. He must appear contrite. He composed himself and walked towards her.

'There's no need to look so smug,' she said. 'You've got some sort of brown gunk on your tie.'

'Oh.' He looked down at his tie and saw that she was right.

'That'll be a smidgeon of Fig Fruitybrown,' he said, determined not to be put off by any hauteur in his wife's manner. She would, he told himself, be bound to seem a little stand-offish. After all, she would not want to seem to be losing face. That was only natural. 'It's a very smart sort of yoghurt. Made by Ron Brown.'

'You look an absolute fright,' she said. 'And don't come any closer. I'm not in the mood.'

'It's awfully nice to see you,' he said.

'Well, I wish I could say the same about you. I've only come back because Parkinson and I agreed it would be best if I did. For the sake of the Board.'

'Parkinson? The Board?' Bognor felt an unpleasant tingling at the base of the spine. There had been talking behind his back. 'What do you mean? Why have you and Parkinson been talking?'

'Because,' she sighed, 'although you may not think it, we both worry about you. We both know you are God's own oaf and we want to protect you. Heaven knows why, but we do. We also, more to the point, want to protect other people from the harm you can do.'

'Now that is unfair, it really is. I never hurt anyone.'

'Not on purpose, I grant. Maybe. There's no malice in you, Simon, but about as much sense and sensibility as a sponge. Anyway, we can't talk here. I'm cold and I'm wet and we need to go somewhere private because I have something serious to tell you.'

'It's lunch time,' he said. 'Let's go and have lunch.'

'You think food and drink is the answer to everything,' she hissed, shrinking into her Jaeger and hunching her shoulders. The headscarf and the hint of blue at the tip of her nose made her look like a foreign royal at the Badminton Horse Trials. 'Let's just go back to that tatty hotel. If you want lunch you can get it on room service, but frankly I should pass. You look as if you've been on a twenty-four-hour lunch seven days a week for a month at least. What you need is an Alka-Seltzer and some exercise. You make Cyril Smith look like Arnold Schwarzenegger.'

'Oh Monica, honestly.'

'Don't you "Oh Monica" me. You ought to know me well enough by now to know when I'm seriously pissed off with you.'

Bognor took a deep breath and appraised her, sidelong, trying not to meet her eyes. She was right. Now was a time to shut up. She was cross with him. Very. Understandably. She had come back. Despite everything. That was good. She was hooked, but she still had to be wound in and landed or whatever one did with fish. Call him a chauvinist if you like, but he could read his wife. Now was a time for saying nothing beyond the essentials.

'OK,' he said. 'We'll talk at the Talbot.' And he trudged off through the drizzle. Shortly she fell in at his elbow, almost, though not quite, in step. They did not speak as they negotiated the bustle of lunchtime Scarpington with its insatiable shoppers. Even in the Sludgelode Centre they said not a word even when a Hare Krishna yobbo Buddhist handed Bognor a sheet of paper inviting him to a free vegetarian lunch at the local temple. It seemed to Bognor even less free than most free lunches and he would have liked to have said so. But one tentative glance at the set of his wife's jaw and the unblinkingness of her eyes was enough to tell him to stay mute.

Only in his room – their room – when they had taken off their sodden outer garments and the Jolly Trencherman do-it-yourself teamaker was plugged in and turned on, did Bognor dare speak.

'Well?' he essayed.

'You're such a prune,' she said.

He did not rise to the bait but broke open a couple of Earl Grey teabags instead.

'It's Wartnaby,' she said, at last. 'There's no such thing.'

'Don't be ridiculous. He brings me breakfast.'

'Whatever.' She kicked off her shoes and tucked her feet up on the bed. 'He's not a policeman and Parkinson has never met him in his life. Parkinson doesn't know Chelsea porcelain from Tuppaware. Wartnaby is a chimera. He's a grotesque product of the imagination. He doesn't exist.'

Bognor counted to ten under his breath.

'Now come on, Monica,' he said. 'You saw him. You listened to him. You bandied quotations with him. You rather liked him. Now, since then he has twice brought me breakfast and he has convinced me beyond a peradventure that he is fighting a lone crusade against local corruption on a scale which you could hardly dream of. And which, to be honest, is of such a squalid nature that I do not think I could reveal it to you.'

The kettle boiled. Bognor made two cups of Earl Grey. One bag, one cup. This was a true marital stand-off. They couldn't even share a pot.

'The fact is,' Monica sipped her tea and wrinkled her aquiline nose, 'to take one fact at a time, that when I mentioned the name Wartnaby and linked it to Chelsea china Parkinson did not react. Wartnaby rang no bell. Nor did Chelsea. He thinks Chelsea is a football team. Or the King's Road.'

'OK.' Bognor tried to keep any strain or tension out of his voice. 'Then how do you explain Wartnaby's story?'

'A combination of scrupulous research and massive chutzpah,' said Monica. 'Homework and nerve – the twin attributes of the con-man through the ages.'

'All right, all right.' Bognor realised that he was beginning to pace. Always a bad sign. 'So Wartnaby didn't meet Parkinson when he was giving a lecture on Chelsea ware. So?'

'So,' said Monica, 'he told a lie.'

Bognor took too big a mouthful of tea, half choked, attempted to cover his confusion by staring out of the window, failed, turned back and conceded.

'So he didn't tell the truth. But he probably had an ulterior motive. He's up against a very nasty conspiracy here: the mafia of middle England. Only worse. You sometimes have to tell little lies to arrive at a greater truth.'

'Oh ha bloody ha!' If Monica had been smoking still she would have exhaled an Olympic concentricity of interlocking rings through both nostrils. 'Parkinson rang the Fenlandshire Constabulary. Do they have a DCI Wartnaby on their books. Do they hell!'

'He's been suspended,' said Bognor, 'so he's not on their

books. And so they would deny all knowledge, wouldn't they? You don't seem to understand. We're talking corruption here. Corruption from the neck up. This is not your cosy, comfy, Golden Age, after-you-Claude, decorous, English by numbers drawing-room comedy of errors garbage. This is genuine nastiness: sex in the afternoon; death after dinner. And the top cops are all part of it. They hate Wartnaby. He threatens them. Be your age. They're trying to use you.'

For a second Bognor thought he detected a tremor of common sense. But then she asked, in all seriousness, 'What makes you think he's who he says he is?'

'Oh God!' He needed something stronger than Earl Grey.

'Listen,' he said, 'Sir Seymour Puce is a bad lot. Every single thing that I've learned since arriving in this God-forsaken dump confirms that view. He makes Al Capone look like Mother Theresa. Surely you accept that?'

Monica, incredibly to him, showed every sign of being as exasperated with him as he was with her.

'I don't think you are listening to me,' she said, very slowly. 'I am telling you that Parkinson, your boss whom you respect, telephoned the Fenlandshire Constabulary, that is to say the local police force here in this part of the world, and they deny all knowledge of anyone answering to the name of Detective Chief Inspector Wartnaby.'

'And I,' said Bognor, 'do not believe you can have been listening to me. I have tried to explain to you that the city of Scarpington is a moral cesspool dominated by the Artisans who turn out to be a very nasty semi-secret society of which everyone in town who matters is a member. The dominant figure in the society is Sir Seymour Puce who is a villain. Every time I uncover some new unpleasantness Puce seems to be at the bottom of it. The Chief Constable is just one among many who are in Puce's pocket. He is blocking the investigation into who killed Reg Brackett and into who killed Freddie Grimaldi and he has had Wartnaby taken off the case and suspended.'

'How do you know all this?'

For the first time Bognor almost faltered.

'Because Wartnaby told me,' he said.

'Exactly.' Monica's expression said 'I told you so'.

'And how do *you* know otherwise?' It was, in Bognor's eyes, one person's word against another's. And he knew who he trusted.

'First, because Parkinson denies ever having met Wartnaby or knowing anything about porcelain. And second because the police say he doesn't exist.'

'Of course the police say he doesn't exist,' said Bognor. 'They're totally corrupt, like everything else in town. He's an unperson because he has dared to meddle in the affairs of the Artisans and he is getting too close for comfort. So they're closing ranks.'

'Then how do you explain Parkinson?'

'Parkinson's getting old. It's time he moved over for a younger man. He must have forgotten.'

Monica stood up and put her shoes back on. 'God, you're impossible,' she said.

'You too.' Bognor was not going to put up with this, he really wasn't. She had not been sleuthing round Scarpington like he had. She had not seen The Laurels. She had not caught the malodorous stench of corruption which clung to Puce and which penetrated everything he touched.

'Your trouble, Monica,' he said, 'is that you just can't bear to be proved wrong. You see. We'll have the definitive answer soon enough. Once Wartnaby confronts Puce in his lair all will be revealed. He won't have a leg to stand on. Between us we'll solve the murders and clean up the Augean stables too.'

'Parkinson was also told that the post-mortem on Brackett showed nothing to suggest that he didn't die from a heart attack,' said Monica, 'and Grimaldi died as the result of smoke inhalation. The police say there's no reason to suspect foul play.'

Bognor was almost ill with exasperation. 'Well, they would, wouldn't they?'

Monica was almost beyond speech. Her moan of anguish

was not in the dictionary though its meaning was quite clear. Then, composing herself, she put on her mac and scarf and started for the door.

'And I can't think what makes you assume that there is ever going to be any kind of confrontation between Wartnaby – always assuming that's his real name – and Puce. My very strong suspicion is that your friend Wartnaby is simply going to vanish into thin air.'

'That's just where you're wrong.' Bognor played his ace with a sang-froid which he knew would irritate but which he could not resist. 'As a matter of fact I have engineered just such a meeting for this very evening. Six o'clock at The Laurels. Gin and tonics at dusk. It should be very revealing.'

Monica looked at him but Bognor had seen the look before and remained standing.

'Where are you going?' he asked as she placed her hand on the doorknob.

'Out,' she said, and was gone.

There was nothing so bleak, in Bognor's experience, as a hotel bedroom with only one person in it. Particularly if the surviving incumbent was in the right. Which he always was. How could one's wife be so wrong? Why were women so perverse? Why was it that when the writing was on the wall only he could read it? Why, oh why?

He fished out the piece of paper with Wartnaby's phone number on it. A curious sensation, knowing that there would be no answer to his call but that Wartnaby – or the man calling himself Wartnaby – would be sitting there watching the receiver, listening to the rings, counting. But not answering.

He dialled '9', waited for the outside line and dialled the Wartnaby number, waited, heard it ring, let it sound six times, then crashed the receiver back into its cradle. Message delivered. Six o'clock at The Laurels, Wedgwood Benn Gardens. There and then all would be resolved.

There was an afternoon to kill and he wasn't sure how to kill it. Sleep was the obvious answer. He needed rest if he was to be on tip-top form and yet, perverse as always, his brain was awash with adrenalin. How often when he had needed to be alert had he been let down by human biology and vice versa? Too often in his career he had been comatose when under threat and on tenterhooks when safe. What was it about him that made him always in the wrong place at the wrong time? Sometimes he felt that he was not cut out for life. Or not, at least, for life as it was lived in this last quarter of the twentieth century. Born a couple of hundred years too late, that was his problem.

His eyes traversed the room. The Gideons' Bible? What's On in Scarpington? The telephone directory? The telephone directory. Why was it that one so often overlooked the obvious? One spent so much time teasing the impossible from the inscrutable, barking up the wrong monkey puzzles, constructing abstruse hypothetical formulae to explain flawed alibis or contradictory motives. One, well, some, were trying to harness the computer for forensic motives, logging into Californian data banks, accessing Scotland Yard, doing things with modems. And then there was DNA and genetic fingerprinting. But so often sophistication merely obscured the simple facts that stared you in the face. In matters of deduction and detection Bognor knew there was no substitute for toil and sweat and never overlooking the bloody obvious when it was sitting there right under your nose. It was too easy for one to be too clever by half.

He sidled over to the phone book. Just suppose, he said to himself, that Wartnaby, as Monica suggests, does not exist. Then he will not be in the phone book. He could, of course, be ex-directory but that wouldn't be in keeping with his persona as presented thus far. All open and above board, that was the DCI Wartnaby he had come to know and, no, love was wrong. But admire, yes. One always admired a crusader.

He flipped the pages. There were a lot of Ws. It was a popular letter. W was for Water Board, now privatised, W was for Warren and Waterbed . . . Waterbed, now there was a . . . hang on, he'd gone too far . . . W was for Wartnaby and Glory Be, W was for Wartnaby and not just for Wartnaby but for Wartnaby O. He could hear the voice of his boss and mentor Parkinson, disembodied, speaking to him from the long long ago. 'Back to the basics, Bognor, back to the basics.' And here he was back at the most basic tool of his trade, the boring old basic first essential tool of the investigator's trade. The phone book. Wartnaby O. 35 Magnolia Avenue. 342.1743. Battle of Dettingen, 1743, he remembered. The last time an English king had led his troops into battle. How tenaciously the least wanted facts of one's education hung around in the mental attic!

He referred to the crumpled paper on which Detective Chief Inspector Wartnaby had written the number for him to ring. It was, as he had half expected, a different number altogether. Curiouser and curiouser.

342 Dettingen seemed to ring for ever. He was on the verge of giving up when a woman's voice answered, thin and quavery. 'Three four two one seven four three, the Wartnaby residence.'

'Is that Mr Wartnaby's home? Mr Osbert Wartnaby?'

'It is.'

'May I speak to him, please?'

'He's still having his nap.' The woman sounded as if Bognor should have realised this. Reproof infected the information. 'If it's very urgent I could see if he's awake. Or perhaps you'd prefer to call back.'

'If he's awake,' said Bognor, 'I'd prefer to talk to him now. If you don't mind.'

'One moment.'

She sounded like a housekeeper, not a wife. But why on earth would Wartnaby be having a nap? Well, a one-off nap was excusable, but a regular daily nap was odd. Wartnaby didn't strike Bognor as the sort of person who would need daily afternoon kips. Rather the reverse.

'Wartnaby'. This voice was thinner and more quavery than the housekeeper's. Quite unlike the brisk, cheery tones of DCI Wartnaby.

'Mr Osbert Wartnaby?'

'Mr Osbert Wartnaby speaking.'

Bognor was confused. Perhaps this was his Osbert Wartnaby's father.

'I'm sorry, but are you by any chance the father of Detective Chief Inspector Wartnaby?'

He realised as soon as he had said it that if the Osbert Wartnaby to whom he was speaking was not aware of his police namesake then the question would sound odd.

This Wartnaby clearly did find the question peculiar.

'Is this some kind of joke?' he asked. If so he implied he didn't think it funny.

'No,' said Bognor. 'It's not a joke at all. I'm trying to trace a friend of mine called Osbert Wartnaby.'

'I think you have a wrong number.' Decidedly testy now.

'No, no.' Bognor did not want him to ring off. 'It's the right number. Just the wrong person.'

He did ring off.

Damn and blast. He sat down hard on the bed and ran a hand through thinning hair which he really must get Monica to cut. If Monica would ever cut his hair again. What to do? Phone again? No point. The geriatric Wartnaby of Magnolia Avenue or his housekeeper would hang up as soon as he breathed, then report him to British Telecom for committing a nuisance over the public wires. Magnolia Avenue. Of course. He had the address. A cab, a cab. He put on his mac and hurried forth on yet another voyage of discovery and missing by no more than five minutes a very important call from his boss, Parkinson, who was in a fine rage before making it and a finer still when there was no answer from Bognor's room.

The Wartnaby residence was the end of a Victorian terrace half-way out towards the Bog. There were tell-tale signs of modest yuppification in some of the other houses – carriage lamps, brass dolphin knockers, out-of-place bow windows with bottle-bottom panes of glass – but number thirty-five looked as if nothing much had been done to it this century. The window sills were peeling and split, an upstairs window had one broken pane filled with cardboard and Sellotape, the guttering had come adrift just above the front door so that a moss green streak ran down the wall to one side, several tiles were missing from the roof and the net curtains were off-grey. Bognor pressed the bell, heard nothing and knocked loudly instead.

Presently the door opened and a thin woman in carpet slippers and a flowered pinafore over a grey skirt and beige cardy told him the house was not for sale. She had a wispy grey moustache and a dew-drop on the end of her nose.

'I came to see Mr Wartnaby.'

'Do you have an appointment?'

'No, but it's very important. I'm from the Board of Trade.' He produced his plastic ID and waved it under her weeping nose.

'Mr Wartnaby won't see anyone without an appointment.'

From the inside of the house a quavering voice called, 'If it's the headmaster, Mrs Simkiss, show him in, show him in.'

'It's not,' Mrs Simkiss called back. 'It's a stranger.'

Bognor put one foot in the door and was startled by a nasty growl from behind Mrs Simkiss's thick-stockinged knees. A dreadful mangy mongrel stood there, snout peeled back over yellow rabid teeth.

'Bonzo bites,' said Mrs Simkiss.

'If it's about the football pools I'd like to talk to him,' called Wartnaby.

'Is it about the football pools?' Mrs Simkiss asked.

'Er . . .' said Bognor. 'It's exceedingly important.' He was getting wet.

'Oh, very well.' Mrs Simkiss's capitulation was sudden and unexpected. 'You'd better come in. Bonzo, leave the gentleman alone.'

Bonzo did some more heavy-duty growling but did not bite. Bognor stepped off the pavement and into a house where time had stood still for at least twenty years. The smell was a musty mix of boiled vegetable vapours and carpet impregnated with urine, presumably Bonzo's. The walls of the hall – more of a corridor than a proper hall –

were covered in peeling paper of the darkest tobacco brown and there were pictures everywhere. Most of them looked as if they had been cut from old issues of the *Illustrated London News*. There were a great many of King Edward VII, one of Lord Kitchener, another of Lord Haig, several ocean liners of *Lusitania* vintage.

Mrs Simkiss shut the door behind him and ushered him into a room off this passage. This too was dark brown with more pictures of a similar kind plus a number of school photographs – some those enormous long thin ones with hundreds of suits, others of rugby and cricket teams. On top of one or two were old caps, some hooped, others little fez-type football ones with gold braid and tassels and small peaks. All over the floor were piles of yellow newspapers tied with string. There was so much furniture that it resembled nothing as much as a junk shop. An extraordinary jostle of occasional tables, a dining-room table, and three battered chaise-longues. On one of these, originally upholstered in bottle green but so stained with wine and food and ink that it resembled a patchwork quilt, there reclined a very old man indeed. His lower half was covered in a tartan rug and his upper was wearing a dark grey suit with waistcoat. He wore a stiff white wing collar and a dark blue tie with a pearl pin. His face had the cadaverous, ultra-wrinkled texture of lizard-skin.

'Mr Wartnaby?'

'I don't recognise you, boy,' said Mr Wartnaby. 'Stand by the window so I can see you properly.'

Bognor, startled, stood in the window. 'It's not Festing Two, is it?' asked Wartnaby. 'I taught your father. Very idle boy. Very idle boy indeed. Caned him for idleness. Gave him lines. Made him learn Lars Porsenna but none of it made the slightest difference. I don't suppose he came to any good.'

Bognor was appalled to find himself half transformed to the schoolroom of thirty and more years ago.

'Actually, sir,' he said, 'I'm not Festing. My name's Bognor.'

'Bognor ... Bognor ... no, I don't think so. I don't

171

remember a boy named Bognor. There must be some mistake. My memory's not what it was. Will you take a glass of Madeira? Mrs Simkiss, two glasses of Madeira, if you please. It isn't often that we're honoured with a visitor. To what do we owe the honour, Mr Bognor?'

With exceedingly ill grace Mrs Simkiss poured amber liquid from a decanter, opaque and grey with neglect, into two glasses which also looked as if they had never been washed. They seemed to Bognor to have a definite patina of years of spittle and Madeira.

'I . . .' said Bognor, and dried. He tried again. 'I'm from the Special Investigations Department of the Board of Trade,' he said, hideously aware that as opening gambits went this was worse than useless. Who was this Wartnaby? What had he got to do with the other Wartnaby? He glanced at one of the photographs. It contained about seventy boys sitting in front of an imitation Colditz Castle only with more drainpipes. Underneath there was a crest and, in Gothick, 'Wartnaby's 1956'.

The penny dropped. In the middle of the seated prefects there was a middle-aged gent in tweed jacket and striped tie who was almost certainly Wartnaby, forty years yon. Well, getting on for forty. On his right the starchy woman with the white matron's cap was Mrs Simkiss also minus forty. Wartnaby was Scarpington's Mr Chips, fallen on hard times, housekept by Matron. Bognor gazed hard at the boy on Wartnaby's left, an arrogant little sod with a fancy brocade waistcoat and a supercilious expression.

'Puce,' he said out loud. 'That's Puce.'

'Ah,' croaked the figure on the chaise-longue, cradling his wine glass with hands like chicken's feet. 'Puce. Most remarkable boy I ever encountered in my entire school career. A true leader of men.' He slurped some Madeira, spilling some on his shirt front. 'A very very remarkable boy. Remarkable.'

'You must have taught Moulton and Festing and Brackett and Brown?'

Bognor seemed to be through the crisis of establishing

his own identity. Wartnaby was up and running through his past. All he needed was a prompt. It didn't matter where it came from. Or from whom. 'Moulton was surprisingly good at geography and he won the shot-putt in '58,' he quavered, 'but he would not clean his shoes. Time and again I had to beat him for not cleaning his shoes. Festing was a grubby little boy. Grubby in mind, grubby in body. Went on to the varsity, though. "Festing," I used to say, "if you go on festing like that you'll festle away into nothing at all."' He cackled. 'But Puce was a fine boy. Even as a new bug he had so much character. Character with a capital "C". I told the headmaster that very first term. "Headmaster," I said, "we have a very remarkable boy in the school. He is only thirteen years old but already he has more leadership qualities than boys of twice his age. He will do great things for Scarpington." And so he has. So he has. He's had a very remarkable career. The child is father to the man, I always say, and that was true of Puce. Not what you'd call an intellect but a leader of men right from the very first.'

Bognor subjected the Wartnaby's House photograph to a more detailed scrutiny while debating whether or not to drink his Madeira. He guessed the alcohol should kill most of the germs. So it was probably safe. He might as well let the old boy rabbit on, in the vague hope that he might say something of interest. It was Puce, all right. Three stone and forty years – well, nearer thirty – had made a difference, but if you scraped them away it was Puce to a T. And there was Moulton and there Festing and there . . . Ah! Bognor almost spilled his drink with excitement. There, at the very end of the middle row, that downtrodden boy with the disgruntled expression. He too was familiar. Three breakfasts in a row Bognor had seen the man fathered by this child. This was his Wartnaby.

Very gingerly he removed the photograph from its place on the wall. Dust scattered everywhere and there was a neat rectangle of a different shade of brown where the picture had been. Bognor tiptoed over to the old schoolmaster who was still burbling on. He was not only very old but extremely smelly. Bognor wondered if he had maligned Bonzo.

'I say, sir,' he said, hearing himself also sounding like a reincarnation of a much earlier self, 'who's that, sir?' And he pointed at young Wartnaby sitting on the end of the bench far from Puce and the housemaster and matron and the seats of power.

The old eyes wept with the effort of screwing themselves up to focus. Concentration wrinkled the Auden lines and furrows of that vespertilian countenance. The old man willed himself to remember.

'A very dim boy. A very dim boy indeed. No recollection of him at all. No, wait. His father had an accident. Very tragic. Ran some sort of milk bar and was killed by a car. It's coming back to me. Sad business. Then the mother killed herself. The boy had to leave early. No money, you see. I'd forgotten all about him until this moment. It must be almost thirty-five years. Very sad story, but not a nice boy. Something very spiteful about him. Other boys didn't like him. He was never a boy's boy. Mrs Simkiss, Mrs Simkiss, what was this boy's name, the one who had to leave after his parents died? The father ran a milk bar.'

Mrs Simkiss came to the chaise-longue, bent over the picture and frowned. 'Smith,' she said at last, 'Peter Smith. Not a nice boy at all. A bed-wetter. Right up until the time he left.'

CHAPTER TEN

'An answer is always a form of death' (John Fowles, *The Magus*)

Puce was already at The Laurels when Bognor arrived. He opened the door to him. The MP was drinking whisky from a Brierley crystal glass. A cigar was smouldering in an ash tray on the hall chest. Puce's smile was fixed but relaxed and he was still in his funereal suiting. He wore it like a hand-fitted carapace. He seemed more than usually impregnable.

'Welcome,' he said, 'to the Artisan Club. You're very privileged. It's rare for us to admit non-members. But as a Board of Trade inspector I suppose you could argue that you are one of us. You'll join me in a Scotch.' This last was an order, not an invitation. Bognor acquiesced and Puce led the way upstairs to the bar with its half-size billiard table and sporting prints.

'We operate an honour system,' said Puce, measuring a double Teachers from the optic. 'The only time we have a barman or any other staff in is when we have some sort of formal gathering here. Which isn't usual. It's a very informal sort of place, as you can see. Take a pew.'

They sat in uncomfortable leather chairs stuffed with horsehair.

'Cheers,' said Puce. 'What can I do for you? I'm a busy man. My chauffeur is calling for me in just over half an hour. I hope that'll be long enough.'

'Cheers.' Bognor took out his notebook. 'That'll be fine. I just wanted to see where it all happened and to ask you one or two questions for my report. Partly about you and partly about the Artisans.'

'Fire away!' Puce thrust his chin out like Mussolini. It was a gesture of symbolic defiance. It said 'Sock it to me, Sunshine. Me Tyson, you Bruno.' Bognor wondered if there was any chance of denting the ego. He was afraid not.

'I'm interested in the amount of power you exert in this town, Sir Seymour,' he began. 'Everywhere I turn you seem either to own the company or be the chairman or a close personal friend of the owner or the chairman. Even here in the Artisans everyone concedes that you're the one who calls the shots.'

Sir Seymour allowed himself a smirk of self-satisfaction. If all the questions were going to be as doddly as this he was going to have no problem.

'It's true that I have a certain position in Scarpington,' he said, 'but as the Member of Parliament I believe passionately that I am elected by my constituents to represent them in Parliament and to do my best to look after their interests. I am in a very real sense a servant of the people. As is any MP.'

Bognor scribbled. He wanted to seem deferential, at least for a while.

'For a servant of the people you're remarkably rich and powerful.'

'I've worked hard all my life to build up a series of highly successful companies. This is a capitalist country, thank God. We're more prosperous than we've ever been in Britain and in Scarpington. When I was a lad I remember men coming to watch football at the Bog in clogs. There's none of that any longer and I take pride in it. Pride and some credit.'

Bognor decided to try a gear change.

'We at the Board,' he said, 'are interested in what makes the British businessman tick. It's why I'm here. Now, obviously, like you he's interested in profit, a high standard of living, company cars, all that kind of thing. But I wonder where the Honours system fits into all this?'

Was it Bognor's imagination or did the great man suck a

little harder on the fat cigar before answering this. Not that it was a very interesting answer.

'How do you mean?' was what he said.

'You have a knighthood,' said Bognor. 'I wondered to what extent your career and behaviour have been dominated by the possibility of becoming Sir Seymour.'

'My knighthood was for "political services". Nothing to do with business.'

'Or money?'

'Or money.'

Sir Seymour's eyes were narrowing.

'Reg Brackett had an MBE.'

'For services to charity. Reginald was a fine man. He did a great deal of very splendid work for the poor and underprivileged of this city.'

'For which he got an MBE.'

'That's the way we do things in this country. We reward those who perform exceptional services over and above the normal. Reg did. So he got his MBE.'

'Nothing to do with twenty thousand pounds? Or services rendered?'

'Just what are you getting at?'

'I'm suggesting that in Scarpington honours are for sale. To be precise, I'm suggesting that you are selling them. I have one informant who claims that he has paid you a large sum of money in return for a guaranteed gong in next year's New Year's Honours.'

'Poppycock!'

'He sounded pretty convincing to me. In any case,' Bognor smiled a sickly smile intended to ingratiate, 'we're men of the world, Sir Seymour. And the Board takes a thoroughly pragmatic view of life. If it works, then it works. If an "honour" can be shown to have a material value, then we at the Board like it. The Board of Trade is not about ethics or morality. It's about the facts of life, money making the world go round. If selling honours makes Scarpington more efficient in the market-place, at the point of sale; if it *works*, then, frankly, it's OK by us.'

'Very neatly put, Simon.' Sir Seymour exhaled. 'You had me worried for a moment. I thought I'd misread you. I didn't take you for a ginger-beard pinko.'

'I should jolly well hope not.' Actually, Bognor did like to think of himself as pinkish, if not ginger-bearded. 'The point is that if selling honours works in Scarpington then it might work elsewhere. It may be being done elsewhere, but in a discreet way we could push the notion around, suggest ways in which it could be done. And so on. It would have to be discreet. I don't think the powers-that-be would be prepared to go public on it. For the Honours System to work it has to be perceived to be squeaky clean while actually being corrupt.'

'Corrupt is not the most fortunate choice of word,' said Sir Seymour.

'No,' said Bognor. 'What I mean is that the Honours System has to be seen by the great unwashed as a sort of airy-fairy way of rewarding life's goody-goodies whereas to those in the know it is actually a ruthlessly gritty commercial enterprise.'

Sir Seymour's smile widened to take in his ears, though not his eyes.

'You must dine with me at the House one night,' he said. 'I think we might be able to develop some interesting commercial projects. I've often felt that the Board of Trade and private enterprise should enjoy a more intimate relationship.'

Bognor simpered back. He wondered where Wartnaby was. Or Smith or whoever he really was. He felt he was shouldering too much of this particular burden. He needed rescuing. He was John Wayne again, surrounded by the Apache, waiting for the bugle call which would signal the relief by US Cavalry. Attack, he knew, was the best defence, so he plunged in.

'Talking of intimate relationships,' he said, 'I wanted to discuss the place of cards in commerce; of bridge as a vehicle of communication within the trading community: the way in which the play and work ethic co-mingle. In short,' he paused and flashed another winsome smile, 'I wanted to learn a little more about the Artisans' Bridge Club.'

Silence. Then, unexpectedly, Sir Seymour said, very slowly, 'A thing well bought is half sold.'

'I'm sorry.' Bognor did not understand.

'An old business adage,' said Sir Seymour, 'like the one about putting business before pleasure. Not that I agree with that. To me the two have always seemed entirely and desirably compatible. I'd go further. There can be no business without pleasure.'

'But you can have pleasure without business.'

Sir Seymour smiled. 'Maybe you can. For myself I have never discovered the secret.'

'So the Bridge Club,' said Bognor, 'is part of the business life of the community.'

'It beats golf,' said Sir Seymour. 'Now let's stop beating about the bush. Nigel Festing told me about your breaking in here and your questions. One or two other Artisans have told me about what you've been asking. I have a strong suspicion that you're exceeding your role.'

Bognor was not having this. 'Board of Trade Investigators have almost totally unfettered powers,' he said evenly.

'Murder,' said Puce, 'is a police matter.'

'Who said anything about murder?'

Despite what he felt was an exemplary exterior appearance of calm, Bognor was internally quite rattled.

'I did,' said Puce.

Oh God, thought Bognor. Bluntspeak. That terrible northern capacity for calling spades shovels. They called it speaking their mind but in Bognor's experience it was largely an excuse for being rude and obnoxious. Like many of his ilk, Bognor believed that little white lies made the world go round.

Puce continued in like manner. 'I believe you think that there was something sinister about poor Reg Brackett's death. And about Freddie Grimaldi. It's not altogether surprising, I admit, but the police have made enquiries and they are satisfied in both instances that there is no question of foul play. I have the Chief Constable's word.'

Naturally, thought Bognor. He was beginning to feel out of his depth. He wished Wartnaby would show up. Then everything would be resolved and he could live happily ever after. At least, that was his theory.

'I assure you,' said Bognor, 'that all I am concerned with is the compilation of my report on the workings of the Scarpington business community. I admit that two deaths immediately after my arrival were unexpected and suspicious. I also have to say that I have discovered a number of things about the business community here which are, well, let's just say that I've been a bit surprised. And I would like to know more about how the Bridge Club works.' He was dimly aware that he was sounding both pompous and lame. A not inconsiderable achievement. He was also having doubts about Puce. Corrupt, certainly, but was he criminal? And above all, was he a murderer? He seemed to be managing perfectly well without having to kill people.

Puce shrugged. 'Well,' he said, 'since we're here I'll show you. It's perfectly straightforward.'

He stood and led the way upstairs. Once inside the door of the Bridge Club there was a strong smell of perfume and the burning hay aroma that could have been an old herbal cigarette but was more likely to have been marijuana.

'I know who that will have been,' said Puce, waving his cigar. 'I keep warning members about narcotics.'

He shoved open the door of the black bedroom. 'It's all quite straightforward,' he said. 'Each session is an hour long. Judges' decision is final.' He sat on the waterbed which wobbled like jelly. 'Not sure about the waterbeds,' he said, 'but the committee were keen. I don't personally think it's done anything for the general level of play. It's like cricketers always going on about whether or not to cover wickets or all that soccer nonsense about plastic turf. There'll never be plastic at the Bog while I'm in charge. And personally I'd go back to traditional mattresses. But then as I'm a non-combatant my views shouldn't in all honesty prevail.'

'Non-combatant?' Bognor had been wondering.

'Let's just say we all get our pleasures in . . . what the hell?' Puce made to stand but sat back hard and rapidly. 'Smith!' he said. 'What in God's name are you doing here?'

It was – of course – Wartnaby. And he had a gun in his hand.

'For God's sake, Wartnaby, put that thing down!' Bognor was seriously agitated.

'Oh, shut up!' said Wartnaby, 'you absolute ass.'

'I am not an absolute ass and I suggest you put that gun down at once before something silly happens which you'll regret.'

Puce's expression suggested that he at least agreed with Smith/Wartnaby's verdict on Bognor's asininity.

'I told Mr Bognor my name was Osbert Wartnaby,' said Smith. 'Rather a good joke, I thought. In the circumstances.' He glanced at Bognor without allowing the gun, pointed straight at Puce's second shirt button, to wobble. 'He was our housemaster. Took a great shine to Puce here, but rather less to me. A great beater of boys and a very nasty piece of work.'

'So you're not a policeman?' Bognor had always been told that he should not be afraid to ask the obvious question.

'Certainly not!' He laughed. 'Detective Chief Inspector Osbert Wartnaby. Not a bad joke, eh, Puce? Not a bad joke. A policeman is a burglar who has retired from practice. That's Proust, Puce. Don't suppose you ever read Proust even though you did go to university. Unlike some. Not that I was ever a burglar. Socially respectable crime has always been my forte – fraud, old lady's legacies, credit card fiddles, even a little subtly contrived extortion. Do you know I successfully passed myself off as the British Ambassador in Manila once? Mind you, Imelda was immensely gullible!

'Much of what I told you was the truth, Simon, sweetie. I've travelled the world on the strength of my minor public school education, and what an advantage it's been. The word of a not-quite-English-gentleman is still considered his bond. Which, of course, accounts in part for Puce's success.

181

Find a half-decent barrow boy, put a plum in his mouth and a striped tie round his neck, and you've got a success on your hands. Forget meritocracy, that's all my eye.'

'I don't understand,' said Bognor, feebly. 'Why didn't you stay abroad?'

Smith/Wartnaby switched the gun towards Bognor, then back to Puce. He looked seriously mad but in a controlled manner that boded no good at all.

'Slights can fester, Simon. In fact the longer you harbour a grudge the worse it gets. That's my experience. They say crime doesn't pay but that's not my experience. Not at all. I put away quite a nest-egg. Not in the Puce league, of course. But enough to live on in some comfort. So I thought to myself, "Smith, old son, why not go home to the land of your fathers, the scenes of your youth, return to your roots and enjoy a happy retirement in the town from which you came?"'

Puce shifted on the waterbed. It wobbled and he wobbled with it. 'Sit still, Puce,' said Smith, 'or I'll shoot you sooner rather than later.'

'You don't have the guts, you little drip,' said Puce. 'You always were a pathetic little man. Age hasn't improved you. If you want to kill me, kill me. Go on. Shoot.'

'That would be far too easy.' Smith leered. 'Undress.'

'Don't be absurd.'

'You too, Bognor. This is going to look as unlike murder as poor little Reg Brackett and Freddie Grimaldi. You're going to be found together naked on a waterbed in a nasty little sex parlour. And one of you will have this gun in his hand. One rubber of bridge which didn't go quite as planned, eh, Puce?'

'I still don't understand.' In part Bognor was playing for time; in part he was genuinely perplexed and really curious.

'What don't you understand?' Smith seemed seriously concerned, anxious that all should be made utterly clear for Bognor's benefit.

'Why you came back. Why you killed Brackett and Grimaldi.'

'Did I say that? How careless. Not that I quite killed Brackett. Just slipped a little atropine in his drink before dinner. Odourless and colourless, no taste. Marvellous stuff if the victim has a dodgy heart already, especially if he's going through something as stressful as an after-dinner speech.'

'But why?' asked Bognor. 'I don't understand why.'

'Let's just say "revenge", let's just say "revenge". Thus the sweet whirligig of time brings in his revenges. Remember doing *Twelfth Night* with Wartnaby, Puce? Knew it word for word, didn't he? Didn't he?'

Puce's face was even more purple than usual. There was no question of fear draining the cherry red from his cheeks. Instead anger was making him incandescent.

'He was always a little crawler,' he said, addressing Bognor as if Smith was not in the room, 'always sucking up and trying to ingratiate himself. Never worked, of course. He was one of nature's also-rans. So he ran away from school and Scarpington and became a small-time crook as he's told us. And eventually when he'd put together a few miserable bob, he came whimpering back and tried to worm his way into Scarpington society. Fat chance. But we fell over backwards to accommodate him. After all, he was an Old Scarpingtonian. He was entitled to wear the Old School Tie. We owed him something for that. So we gave him the chance. But he failed the initiation. Failed miserably. A second humiliation, you see. And he can't forgive those of us who failed him.'

'Shut up, Puce! Shut up and undress! You too, Bognor. This is your last warning. I'll count to ten and if you haven't started I'll fire. I'm quite good with this little job. I've come a long way since the school corps. And I'll start with the knees, Puce. Which will be painful. So if I were you I'd get 'em off. Shoes first. One . . . two . . .'

It was best to stall for time. Both victims knew it. There was a real madness in those unblinking eyes and a lifetime of resentment and pent-up hatred, of a truly baleful, demonic chip on the shoulder. After almost fifty-odd years of coming off a bad second best this was Smith's one chance to get even.

Puce started to unlace a shoe. Bognor, still standing, pulled at his tie.

And then, from outside, came the sound of the relieving force. The siege of The Laurels was being lifted. Oddly, it sounded like a woman's voice, though the loudspeaker which amplified it was so messy with the interfering whine and buzz of static that it was difficult to be sure. In any event, if it was a female voice it was deep, bossy and authoritative.

What it said was 'Attention! Attention! This is the police. This is the police. The house is surrounded. We are armed. I repeat, there are armed police outside at both front and back entrances to The Laurels. You have five minutes in which to leave the house by the front door with your arms above your head. If you do not do so within five minutes we shall force an entry. I repeat, we are armed police. If resisted we shall shoot to kill. I repeat, we will shoot to kill.'

Normally Bognor would have been quite critical in his woolly liberal manner at the idea of armed police crawling around Wedgwood Benn Gardens for no good reason at all. He was very worried about the excesses of the modern constabulary and it was disturbing that the Fenlandshire force should be able to field some sort of commando-style SAS squad early on a weekday evening. And for no good reason. Dimly he thought he recognised the dread hand of Parkinson pulling rank and puppet strings from the basement offices of the Board of Trade in Whitehall. In which case he would have a stiff word when he got back. Why couldn't he leave him to get on with the job? Interference like this always led to tears, though to be honest, it might get him out of a slight jam. Smith did seem surprisingly serious.

'Now the other,' he said to Puce, who had actually removed one shoe.

Bognor took off his jacket. Puce started to undo the other shoe-lace.

'Get on with it,' said Smith. 'I haven't got all day.'

'You won't get away with this,' said Puce.

'I wouldn't bet on it.' Smith's lip twitched. 'I shall either effect an escape, or simply say that I heard shots and discovered your bodies.'

'You're mad,' said Bognor.

'I've sometimes wondered about that,' he said, quite seriously. 'I suppose it depends on one's definitions. Samuel Beckett says we're all born mad, only some remain so. I think he's probably right.'

From outside there came another burst on the loudspeaker.

'We shall issue only one more warning. I repeat, there will be only one further warning. After that armed police will enter the building. Anybody obstructing officers in the execution of their duties is liable to be shot on sight. I say again, we are armed police. If you do not come out with your hands above your heads we shall enter the building and, if necessary, shoot to kill.'

'Get on with it,' said Smith, hand beginning to waver slightly. Bognor and Puce looked at each other. The telepathy wasn't there. They didn't know how to overcome Smith without the very real danger that one of them might be shot.

'This *is* cosy,' said Smith. 'Such a cosy way to die, don't you think?' He snickered. 'Do you remember that time you beat me in the dorm, Puce? Beat me in the dorm with my trousers down so that I bled. I've been looking forward to this ever since.'

Puce began to unbutton his shirt. He was as out of condition as Bognor. Fat.

Then things began to happen very fast.

The last warning from the police came quicker than they had anticipated and was very terse and tense as if the constabulary's nerve was beginning to crack. Only seconds later there was a smash of breaking glass and Bognor heard himself call out, 'They're coming in through the window.' This seemed to panic Smith who glanced momentarily at the window of the black room, as if balaclava'd SAS men might be swinging in on ropes from the monkey puzzle. As he glanced, Sir Seymour bent down and in a movement which must have derived from the days when he fielded at cover in the King's Scarpington First XI he picked up a shoe and threw it at Smith, catching him hard in the midriff. As this happened Smith must have pulled the trigger. There was a sharp crack, a rending sound and then a fierce jet of water shot up from the waterbed. Puce caught this thin pressurised fountain full in the face, but the distraction allowed Bognor to make a clumsy lunge at his would-be assassin. This was brave but dodgy for as he and Smith-Wartnaby collided, the gun went off a second time. Puce let out a strange, high-pitched shriek and sank beneath a tidal wave as the bed collapsed beneath him with a soggy rending noise. Water, water everywhere. Amazing how much of the stuff you needed to fill a bed. Although not in danger of drowning, the Member for Scarpington was soaked. Also wounded. Blood flowed from his wrist and four-letter words from his mouth. It was difficult to be sure whether pain or indignity was afflicting him most. He was obviously feeling hurt and silly. Bognor stared at him, not at all sure what to do, and in this moment of slack-jawed inertia the gunman, disarmed now, for the weapon had fallen to the floor, was off and away down the stairs. The two almost naked men stayed stunned like a couple of jellyfish stranded on the pebbles by the ebbing tide. Screams. Shouts. They both rushed out and down to the landing, Puce dripping blood from his hand. And on the landing, on a flowered Axminster, they found Smith lying flat out, staring up with extraordinary malevolence at a single assailant, one of whose knees rested threateningly on his jugular, another on his groin, while the hands pinioned Smith's arms in some sort of rudimentary half-nelson.

It was Monica, Mrs Bognor. On her own.

'Good grief,' said Bognor. 'Monica.'

'Go and find something to tie him up with,' she ordered. 'And for God's sake put some trousers on. You both look preposterous and frankly rather revolting.'

*

At least Sir Seymour had the grace to give them a late dinner at the Talbot that evening. His hand was heavily bandaged, though it was only a surface wound. They had Dom Perignon and a bucket of his personal Beluga from the cold store.

'Frankly,' he said, 'I didn't think the little wanker had it in him. The police surgeon didn't seem to know anything about atropine.' A bottle of this had been found in Smith's flat at Sludgelode Mansions. He had nicked it from the pharmacy at Scarpington General simply by breezing in wearing a white coat and carrying a clipboard. People tended to forget, thought Bognor, that the basis of being a confidence trickster was not so much winning confidence as exhibiting it. Walk around as if you owned the place and most people would believe you did. 'And the bruise on Grimaldi's temple was perfectly consistent with his falling over and hitting his head on the grate. And the fire *was* started with a cigarette.'

'Tell me,' said Monica, 'I mean, I don't wish to seem crude but was he really too bad to pass your entry exam?'

'Brackett and Grimaldi and I all marked him quite separately and put our score in sealed envelopes. When we opened them we had all given him nought out of ten. He didn't like it when we told him. But we interviewed his partner or opponent, call her what you will. She's a professional lady we use on these occasions and have for a good many years. She confirmed our view. Nought out of ten. No question.'

'Dear, dear,' said Monica, helping herself to some more caviar.

'It was awfully brave of you to come on your own,' said Bognor, 'and an inspired touch to hire that loud-hailer.'

Monica flashed him a glance which said, 'Shut up you fat, dissolute ass.'

'Police just laughed,' she said. 'I couldn't get past the sergeant on the desk, and, as you know, the desk sergeant is a pretty low form of life. So I had to come on my own. It was perfectly obvious that you two wouldn't be able to cope.'

Both men winced.

'I don't suppose,' said Puce, 'that you'd contemplate honorary membership of the Artisans Mrs Bognor? We'd waive the entry requirements, of course. I have a feeling you might fit in rather well. We're always on the look-out for new blood.'

Mrs Bognor turned to the MP and looked down her nose as if from a very great height indeed. 'Sir Seymour,' she said, 'when my husband has compiled his report on the business activities of this community, I shall recommend to Mr Parkinson that he be sent to investigate Britain's Women's Institutes with special reference to flower arrangement, origami and the place of the rock cake in our national cuisine. Alternatively Mr Parkinson may decide to send him somewhere a little safer and duller than Scarpington. Beirut, perhaps. I, for my part, have no wish ever to come to this perfectly bloody place, ever again. Even though this is very good caviar and very good champagne.'

'I'm sorry,' said Puce. 'I only asked.'

Bognor, for his part, recognising the symptoms, knew that silence was the better part of valour.

'When a lady's erotic life is vexed, Sir Seymour,' she said, 'God knows what God is coming next.' Then she turned to focus on her husband. 'As for you,' she said, 'I'll talk to you later.'

Jill McGown
A Perfect Match £3.99

The news rocked the town. A woman's body found in a boathouse.
And the woman's last known companion Missing Presumed Fled. To
the people of Stansfield it's an open and shut case.

But Detective Inspector Lloyd – teamed up once more with Sergeant
Judy Hill – isn't so quick to jump to conclusions. To begin with he's
certain of only two things. First, that nothing can stop the
reawakening of his tender feelings towards his colleague.

And second: in a murder inquiry you don't rule *anybody* out . . .

'An absolutely classic Christie-type mystery – all motives and clues
and timetables – done with a beautifully sure hand'
US LIBRARY JOURNAL

'A shapely and intelligent classic murder mystery'
THE MAIL ON SUNDAY

'Compelling' THE SUNDAY TIMES

Simon Brett
Mrs, Presumed Dead

'Living in a house where a murder had taken place did give a certain social cachet . . .'

Intrepid detective Mrs Pargeter, sixtysomething (and a little bit more) has risked almost everything with a daring move to the well to do houseing estate of Smithy's Loam. Yet something rankles about her new neighbours . . .

Do they all have behave as if a body in the fridge is a perfectly *normal* event? Does every bored and lonely housewife have a guilty secret behind the fixed smiles and the endless round of coffee mornings?

As Mrs Pargeter soon comes to realise, Smithy's Loam might be perfect for social climbing . . . but it's also perfect for murder . . .

'Mrs Pargeter is a thoroughly modern Miss Marple' CHICAGO SUN-TIMES

'Entertainingly sharp eyed as it looks over the garden walls'
THE GUARDIAN

'Full of dry wit, keen observation and suspenseful plotting'
FINANCIAL TIMES

All Pan books are available at your local bookshop or newsagent, or can be ordered direct from the publisher. Indicate the number of copies required and fill in the form below.

Send to: **CS Department, Pan Books Ltd., P.O. Box 40,
            Basingstoke, Hants.   RG21 2YT.**

or phone: 0256 469551 (Ansaphone), quoting title, author
            and Credit Card number.

Please enclose a remittance* to the value of the cover price plus: 60p for the first book plus 30p per copy for each additional book ordered to a maximum charge of £2.40 to cover postage and packing.

*Payment may be made in sterling by UK personal cheque, postal order, sterling draft or international money order, made payable to Pan Books Ltd.

Alternatively by Barclaycard/Access:

Card No.

Signature:

Applicable only in the UK and Republic of Ireland.

While every effort is made to keep prices low, it is sometimes necessary to increase prices at short notice. Pan Books reserve the right to show on covers and charge new retail prices which may differ from those advertised in the text or elsewhere.

NAME AND ADDRESS IN BLOCK LETTERS PLEASE:

....

Name ——————————————————————————————

Address ——————————————————————————————

———————————————————————————————————

———————————————————————————————————

———————————————————————————————————

3/87